THE C

A James Acton Thriller

Also by J. Robert Kennedy

James Acton Thrillers

The Protocol

Brass Monkey

Broken Dove

The Templar's Relic

Flags of Sin

The Arab Fall

The Circle of Eight

The Venice Code

Pompeii's Ghosts

Amazon Burning

The Riddle

Blood Relics

Sins of the Titanic

Saint Peter's Soldiers

The Thirteenth Legion

Raging Sun

Wages of Sin

Wrath of the Gods

The Templar's Revenge

The Nazi's Engineer

Atlantis Lost

The Cylon Curse

Special Agent Dylan Kane Thrillers

Rogue Operator

Containment Failure

Cold Warriors

Death to America

Black Widow

The Agenda

Retribution

Delta Force Unleashed Thrillers

Payback

Infidels

The Lazarus Moment

Kill Chain

Forgotten

Templar Detective Thrillers

The Templar Detective

The Templar Detective and the Parisian Adulteress

The Templar Detective and the Sergeant's Secret

Detective Shakespeare Mysteries

Depraved Difference

Tick Tock

The Redeemer

Zander Varga, Vampire Detective

The Turned

THE CYLON CURSE

A James Acton Thriller

J. ROBERT KENNEDY

ISBN-10: 1724276743

ISBN-13: 978-1724276742

First Edition

10 9 8 7 6 5 4 3 2 1

For Malcolm Stone.

You will be missed.

THE CYLON CURSE

A James Acton Thriller

"Lordship for many is no good thing. Let there be one ruler, one king, to whom the son of devious-devising Kronos gives the scepter and right of judgment, to watch over his people."

Homer's Iliad 2.118-206

"It has been said that Democracy is the worst form of government except all those other forms that have been tried from time to time."

Winston Churchill, 1947

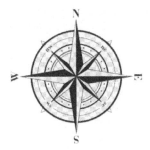

AUTHOR'S NOTE

Cylon of Athens is an actual figure from history, and is where the inspiration for this novel came from, not the television series Battlestar Galactica created by Glen A. Larson, inspired, I assume, by the same source material.

PREFACE

What we now refer to as Ancient Greece, during the time of Cylon, was, in fact, the city-state of Athens. Nations did not exist, and it was the city or town that exerted control over an area.

Many of these cities were ruled by tyrants. What one must remember, however, is that the definition of tyrant was quite different from today. Today, a tyrant is thought of as someone evil, leading with an iron fist, ignoring the will of the people. In ancient times, a tyrant was someone who usurped control in what we might now call a coup d'état. Yes, often they ruled with an iron fist, though these were different times, and applying our values to events of millennia ago, would be perhaps misguided.

In 632 BC, when the historical events of this novel take place, Athens was experimenting with the first forms of democracy, while city states surrounding them were led by unelected rulers, including the tyrant of Megara, Theagenes, the father-in-law of an Olympic hero and aristocrat, Cylon of Athens.

It was with Theagenes' encouragement that Cylon began an undertaking he was certain was for the good of the city he loved.

And to fulfill a prophecy, as most tend to be, too vague to interpret with certainty.

Phaleron Delta Necropolis

Athens, Greece

Two days from now

Archaeology Professor Laura Palmer sprinted toward the screams of terror and the rattle of gunfire as her husband ushered their two young companions to safety. She couldn't see what was going on, the dig site deep enough that anything beyond its edge was out of sight, but what she heard suggested an attack at the main gate.

An attack fiercely resisted by the newly arrived security team she was funding.

These were her people, and if anything happened to them, she'd be responsible.

Though that notion was foolish.

She rushed up the ramp leading to the parking area and the main gate, staring toward the gunfire. Several of the security team were writhing on the ground, the attackers obviously taking her team by surprise, the others continuing to resist valiantly.

Bile filled her mouth as she spotted one who couldn't possibly be alive, but she had to know. She made for his still form when small bursts of sand and stone tore toward her and she froze for a moment, the scene unfolding as if in slow motion.

"Move!"

Somebody shoved her from behind and she hit the ground hard, the impact bringing her back to reality. She rolled out of the way then cried out as the bullets meant for her tore into the man who had just saved her life. He fell down the ramp and out of sight, and she scrambled toward the open pit to check on him when more gunfire cut off her foolishness. She pushed to her feet and leaped behind a car, using the wheel as cover.

"Professor! Are you okay?"

She glanced over and spotted one of the security team taking cover behind the next car. "Yes." She held out her hand. "Gun!"

He tossed her a Glock and three magazines. "You know how to use that?"

She ignored the question, instead checking the weapon then taking up a prone firing position under the car. She opened fire on anything moving near the front gate, wondering what she must have done in a previous life to deserve this.

Why can't we go anywhere without something going wrong?

Temple of Apollo

Delphi, Ancient Greece

632 BC

Cylon's heart hammered as he climbed the last few steps after waiting all day. He couldn't recall feeling so ill at ease, even when in the thick of Olympic competition in the races. The pressure to win had been tremendous, the relief felt after crossing the finish line victorious, orgasmic.

But this wasn't the Olympics. This wasn't a race against his fellow citizens. This was an audience with Pythia, the high priestess of the Temple of Apollo, known in the whispered halls of Athens as the Oracle of Delphi.

The mystery shrouding her and those who had preceded her was something he had always dismissed as superstition, but as each step brought him closer, the heavy fog billowing out of the ground, the flickering flame that took only the edge off the darkness, and the full moon that lit the night sky, all contributed to his uneasiness.

For what was said in the following moments could change his destiny.

He took the final step and suppressed a gasp at the sight of a woman, covered in the finest cloths, prone on an altar in the center of the temple. A gentle breeze blowing across the hilltop had the shimmering layers she wore fluttering, obscuring her form and features, and he dared not judge whether she was beautiful lest he offend Apollo himself, whose choice in whom to speak for him was no doubt wise.

"High Priestess, Cylon of Athens seeks your guidance."

Cylon flinched at the chorus of voices, only now noticing the dozen priestesses surrounding him, positioned between the pillars supporting the roof of the holy temple.

"What is his question?"

The voice was serpent-like, and he was certain it came from the shadows, or at least echoed from the darkness.

He drew a long, slow breath, calming himself unsuccessfully, then stepped forward. "I seek the guidance of Apollo on this most holy of days. Should I follow my father-in-law's urgings, and seize the reins of power of my great city, and return it to the path of strength and order it has so foolishly forgotten?"

The hissed response was almost immediate. "Theagenes is wise and strong, and the gods respect the power that he wields on their behalf. Your family is one of honor, you are a hero of the people, and should you act wisely, you will succeed in unifying the citizens of Athens. But be warned. Patience is key. Take action not this day, but on the day that honors Zeus. To not heed this warning will result in a tragedy that will haunt you until the day you depart this plane of existence, and journey on to the next."

His chest swelled with pride as his eyes burned with tears that threatened to rush down his face. He had her blessing, and his. Apollo, the god of light, through his Oracle in this world, had assured him of victory, and with the Olympic celebrations occurring next week, there was little doubt that this was when he was to make his move and usurp power from those who would weaken the city he loved.

He bowed deeply. "Thank you for your generous guidance."

"Wait," hissed the voice from in front of him, and from the shadows. "Give him the token."

A priestess emerged from the darkness with her hands extended in front of her. In her palms, she carried a plush purple pillow with a gold, tear-shaped amulet perched in the center. She stopped in front of him, saying nothing.

"Wear this to give you the strength of Apollo. Should you succeed, blessed will be all who wear it. But should you fail, all who possess it shall know nothing but misery."

His hands trembling, he reached out, uncertainly, an internal debate raging on whether he wanted to touch something associated with such a prophecy.

Yet he couldn't refuse.

No one refused a gift from the Oracle.

He picked up the amulet with both hands, holding it above his head. "I thank you, Oracle, for such a generous gift, and will heed your words."

"I grow tired. Leave us."

The writhing form in front of him abruptly collapsed onto the altar, all movement ceasing save her heaving chest, the wind that had kept her robes in motion and the flames' flickering suddenly failing, leaving the curious fog to rise unfettered, enveloping the altar in a shroud of secrecy that had him backing slowly away as the priestesses that had surrounded the proceedings receded into the dark.

He placed the amulet around his neck, rubbing the small token between his thumb and forefinger as he closed his eyes, trying to remember every word that had just been said. He opened his eyes and turned, hurrying down the steps, toward the bottom of the hill and his waiting entourage. And with each step, his confidence grew, and by the time he reached the bottom, he had no doubt that not only was Apollo on his side, but that it was his duty to save his people.

And become Tyrant of Athens.

Dimotiki Agora
Athens, Greece
Present Day

Karan Damos watched as the woman in front of him carefully unwrapped what he hoped would be yet another valuable artifact that he could sell to his collectors. She had provided him with several over the past months, all fetching good prices, his commissions helping his bottom line handsomely.

Too bad it was all illegal.

That didn't bother him, though he suspected it did her. She always seemed uncomfortable, always treated the artifacts with loving care, and always sought assurances from him that they would find a "good home."

He, of course, said all the right things to her, even if he couldn't care less where they ended up.

He wanted the cash they provided, and once in hand, where the artifacts ended up were of no concern to him. Artifacts, iPhones, jewelry, whatever. It was all his business. Some called him a fence, but in his mind, he was simply a purveyor of lost and found goods.

Someone lost something through carelessness, and his suppliers found them.

Then brought their loot to him for their twenty to forty cents on the Euro.

This woman commanded much more, for what she trafficked in was unique. Rare. Priceless in some circles. He had agreed to the unthinkable, taking only a 25% commission on whatever he managed to get.

He could have lied to her, but if he were found out, it could affect his entire business. There was honor among thieves. To a point.

He smiled at the bronze blade in front of him, expertly cleaned, the imperfections of time remaining to add to the authentic feel. No collector wanted truly mint condition. A shiny, perfect blade might as well have been made in a Chinese factory. Something that clearly appeared ancient, however, could command a huge price, especially on the Dark Web auction sites he frequented.

"Beautiful."

She nodded. "It is, isn't it?" She tapped the hilt. "I expect an excellent price for this."

"Of course. It will be auctioned tonight. You'll have your share in the morning as per usual."

"Excellent." She paused, staring about the rear of his small appliance repair shop, a front for his illicit dealings. "I have a more valuable item."

He grinned. "Do you have it with you?"

She shook her head. "No. It will be difficult to obtain, and I want certain assurances before I do."

"Such as?"

"I want seven figures. Minimum."

His eyebrows rose. "It must be quite the item."

"It is. Trust me, there will be a bidding war for this item, I assure you."

His grin grew. "I like the sound of that, but it might take time."

Her eyes narrowed. "Why?"

"Seven figures is too big for me. I'll have to make some calls."

"How long?"

"You should know by tomorrow if your minimum can be met."

"That's fine, but no later. Outside people are being brought in, and once they arrive, it might be too late."

"Why not stick to the small things? Nobody has noticed so far. We've both made a tidy sum. Why risk it on one big score?"

She shook her head. "Somebody *has* noticed. That's why these outsiders are being called." Her fingers drummed on the table several times before ending in a definitive rap. "No. One last item, then I'm done. It will give me all I need."

He frowned. "I'm sorry to hear that. But if you want seven figures, I'm going to need to know what it is I'm selling."

She handed him a memory stick and he plugged it into his computer, a series of photos displayed.

"What am I looking at?"

"Proof of who is buried at the tomb."

His eyes widened as he clicked through the photos. "You've figured it out?"

"We have."

"Who?"

And when he heard, he realized seven figures wouldn't be a problem at all, perhaps even eight.

And that meant a new class of criminal would become involved.

A far more dangerous class than he had ever dealt with.

Cylon Residence

City of Athens

632 BC

Cylon lay on a couch, wine in hand, listening to the impassioned debate of his friends. Stimulating conversation was his favorite pastime, even more so than sport, at which he excelled. As a champion of the Olympics, he was hailed a hero by most of Athens' citizenry, and with his position as a member of one of the aristocratic families, he was shown automatic respect.

But respect with a smile.

The people loved him.

And it was this very reason that started the conversations surrounding the troubles now facing Athens, and the possible solutions he and his friends could bring. He was a public figure, he was loved by the masses, he was handsome, wealthy, and well-married, his father-in-law the tyrant of Megara, a city much better off than it had been before Theagenes' takeover.

Athens wasn't suffering. Not yet. But it would if this foolish notion of granting more power to the citizens were to continue unopposed. At one time, it was only the aristocracy that had a say in the affairs of the city-state. After all, it was the aristocracy that defended the city, that paid for everything the citizenry enjoyed. But with the advent of the *hoplite* soldier, who merely had to provide his own body armor and weapon, and in exchange for fighting for the city was given a say in its affairs, the grip on power people like him had held since time immemorial was slipping away.

And it was well known that the common man was an idiot.

The uneducated masses shouldn't be allowed to hold sway over the affairs that affected people like him, the privileged few who had made this great city what it was today. To suggest that the unwashed masses could do better was an insult to the countless generations before him that had built what the citizenry took for granted.

This notion of people having a say was insulting. It was selfish. It was ignorant.

And it couldn't stand.

The archons leading the city into ruin had to be replaced, replaced by people of strength, of good character, and of good standing. People like him.

"What will you do now that you have Apollo's blessing?"

Cylon regarded his best friend, Basileios. He had known the man since childhood. They had fought countless battles at each other's side, and competed as friendly rivals in the Olympics.

They were inseparable.

Among their friends, it was often said they were brothers of another mother, their similarities so numerous.

He didn't know what he would do without him.

"What would you have me do, my friend?"

Basileios held up his wine. "I would honor the will of the gods." He rose to address those gathered. "My friends, we have been given an opportunity that must not be let to pass. My good friend, my *best* friend, Cylon, has proven time and again that he loves our great city, that he loves its people. He has proven he is a fine warrior, a champion Olympian, and a skilled administrator, his house one of the greatest in our fair city." Basileios paused, surveying those around him. "But he has also shown he is not driven by the ambition that too many who would take power are commanded by. Our good friend here, rather than rush out and seize power, because we urged him to, instead sought the council of Pythia, and was granted a rare audience. He completed the rituals, and passed the tests necessary to actually receive her council, and when asked if he should do that which we have been urging him for months, the Oracle of Apollo herself said yes. And she actually told him when he should do it, on the day that honors Zeus himself." He turned and smiled at Cylon, raising his cup. "To our future leader, Cylon!"

Drinks were raised all around, those gathered chanting his name three times before downing their imbibements. Servants rushed from the periphery, refilling the cups, as Cylon acknowledged the courtesy shown him, then rose, bringing a silence of anticipation.

"Some may doubt what the Oracle said to me. I can understand this, for often what she says is ambiguous. But what is often unclear, what often has more than one meaning, cannot be said of the prophecy given to me. She said, 'should you act wisely, you will succeed in unifying the people of Athens.' And that is what I think we have all been doing. Acting wisely. We have not rushed to a quick decision on what should be done. We have debated this for months, and with Pythia's words, I am certain the decision we have come to is the correct one. But we must still not rush into things. She said 'take action not this day, but on the day that honors Zeus.' She also warned that not doing so would result in tragedy. Though it will require some patience, we must not ignore her warning."

"The next festival honoring Zeus is in three weeks. This will give us time to organize, to make sure the people are on our side when we make a move." Basileios held up his cup, staring at the heavens. "Our god Apollo is truly wise."

Cylon smiled, but shook his head. "He is indeed, but not so much you, I fear."

Gentle laughter swept through the friends, even Basileios joining in. "I bow to your greater wisdom, oh wise one. Please, explain to me how I am the fool."

"The next day that honors the great Zeus is in two days, at the start of the Olympics."

Basileios' eyebrows rose. "Are you sure? I mean, yes, Zeus is of course honored during the opening ceremonies, but the day honors many gods. The Festival of Pandia in three weeks specifically honors our god Zeus, and him alone. This would also give us the time to organize our supporters. Two days simply isn't enough time."

Cylon smiled at his friend's concern. "Your words are wise, my friend, and not those of a fool, I assure you. And if the message had been delivered to anyone else, I might agree with you. But it wasn't. It was delivered to me, not only an Olympian, but an Olympic champion. Surely, Apollo recognized the significance of this. Surely, he meant for me to seize control on the anniversary of my greatest triumph, when the citizenry is filled with the memories of my victory, and their hearts are filled with the joy of sport and competition."

"But—"

Cylon raised a hand, silencing his friend. "And there is one more thing, one more thing I have not yet shared with any of you."

All present leaned forward, including the servants that surrounded them.

He held aside his robe, revealing the amulet given to him by Pythia. "This amulet was given to me as a token by the high priestess herself, after the prophecy was delivered. She said it would give me the strength of Apollo." He paused to let his words sink in, the gasps and excited utterances proving his words were having the desired effect. "Let our followers know of the prophecy, let them know of this gift from the high priestess, and let them know that we are fueled by the power of Apollo in our quest to restore order to our great city!"

Everyone rose to their feet, chanting his name while pumping their fists high in the air.

And goosebumps rippled over his body as he relived his Olympic glory, his chest swelling as he realized that once he took power, the entire city would chant his name for the rest of his days.

"Should you succeed, blessed will be all who wear it. But should you fail, all who possess it shall know nothing but misery."

He suppressed the frown that threatened to spoil the moment as he remembered the rest of what Pythia had said, and the doubt those words brought. For if he did indeed have the power of Apollo behind him, then how could he possibly fail? It was a contradiction that made no sense, and the more he thought about it, the more he was plagued by uncertainty.

Perhaps Basileios was right, and they should delay for several weeks to unite their forces.

But it was too late. To change it now would be to show weakness.

He was committed.

And it could mean the death of him, and everyone he loved.

Granger/Trinh Residence

St. Paul, Maryland

Present Day

Tommy Granger raised his glass rather awkwardly, leaving little doubt the young man wasn't used to drinking from a wine glass. "I'd like to propose a toast."

Archaeology Professor James Acton put down his fork and raised his glass, along with his wife, Laura Palmer, and Tommy's other half, Mai Trinh.

"Umm, ahh, I'm not sure what to say. I think, umm, that this might actually be the first toast I've ever given, but, umm, I'd like to thank you both for coming tonight. You've both been so good to us, so supportive—"

"And fed us countless times!" interjected Mai.

Tommy smiled at her, his eyes revealing the love he had for the young woman. "Too many times!" He returned his attention to their guests. "And now that we have our own place, and we've figured out how to operate all the appliances, we'll start trying to repay you for your kindnesses." He lifted his glass a little higher. "May this be the first of many meals we enjoy together here."

"Hear, hear!" Acton took a drink then put his glass down.

"Well done, Tommy," said Laura. "I would never have guessed that was your first toast."

Tommy blushed. "Well, I did practice a little."

Mai squeezed his hand. "For days!"

Acton laughed. "Well, I remember when I was a kid, I was in Boy Scouts. We had a big jamboree, and I was asked to say grace. We were never that religious growing up, so I had no clue what the heck that was, so when it was time, my Scout Leader nodded at me and I rose, bowing my head along with hundreds of other kids, then said 'Grace.' I sat back down and started to eat. It took me a few moments before I realized everyone was just staring at me, then suddenly the entire place broke out into laughter." He sighed. "You wouldn't believe the number of dishes I had to wash that night."

Laura squeezed the back of his neck. "I *love* that story. 'Grace.' Can you believe it?"

Tommy was grinning, though Acton had a sense that Mai was only joining in out of respect, the young woman, a Vietnamese refugee for all intents and purposes, her exposure to American culture only recent. She was thriving, especially now that Tommy was in her life, but it would take time before she picked up on all the idiosyncrasies that made an American American.

He envied her immersion in a new culture so alien to her own, yet it wasn't all smiles. She missed her family. Terribly. Though with modern technology, and some greased palms of their neighbors, she was able to speak to them from time-to-time using borrowed phones.

She didn't dare call them directly, as the Vietnamese government was not pleased with her. She had sacrificed her future in Vietnam to help strangers in their time of need.

And paid a heavy price.

Though if one were to walk into that small, humble apartment today, and see the joy on her face, one could be forgiven for thinking her past was simply a story told to entertain, rather than the truth.

But he had been there, and so had Laura, and if it weren't for young Mai Trinh, they'd both probably be dead, or worse, in a Vietnamese prison, rotting with the vermin.

"Where are you?"

He flinched. "Huh?"

"You look like you're a million miles away."

Acton smiled at Laura, patting the hand on his shoulder that had shaken him out of his reverie. "Sorry, just remembering how we all met."

Phaser fire erupted from his pocket and he looked down, aghast at having forgotten to put his phone on vibrate. "I'm so sorry." He fished his phone out and checked the number displayed. "Country code thirty. Is that Greece?"

Laura nodded. "I think so. Answer it and find out."

Acton turned to his hosts. "Do you mind?"

Both shook their heads. "Of course not," replied Tommy.

Acton swiped his thumb and pressed the phone against his ear. "Hello?"

"Hi. Is this Jim?"

His eyes narrowed, not recognizing the voice, though the accent confirmed Greece. "Yes, it is. To whom am I speaking?"

The man laughed. "I wouldn't expect you'd recognize my voice after all these years. This is Professor Basil Antoniou, from the University of Athens."

Acton smiled as he pictured the awkward man he hadn't seen in at least five years. "Basil, how are you?"

"I'm well, very well. And you?"

"Still on the right side of the dirt. Married as well." He gave Laura's knee a squeeze.

"Wonderful news, though I was aware. The archaeology world is a small one, and when two of its most prominent members wed, the news is bound to spread."

Acton laughed. "I suppose so. To what do I owe the pleasure?"

"I'm calling to invite you and your lovely wife to Greece. Phaleron Delta to be exact."

Acton's heart skipped a beat as a smile spread across his face. "The necropolis?"

"So, you've heard of it?"

Acton chuckled. "In passing."

It was Antoniou's turn to laugh. "Will you come? I'd love to show you both around."

"Let me confirm with Laura." He held the phone against his chest. "You, me, tomorrow, the Phaleron Delta Necropolis. In?"

"Is a bear Catholic? But make it the day after tomorrow."

He grinned then returned to his call. "How's the day after tomorrow sound?"

"Like someone who has too much time on his hands. Let me know when you're arriving, and I'll meet you at the airport."

"Will do. Thanks for the invite, Basil, I've been dying to see what you guys have found."

"It's breathtaking, Jim, absolutely breathtaking." He sighed. "And heartbreaking."

Acton frowned, picturing the images splashed across the newspapers worldwide only recently. "It is, indeed. Have you figured out who they are?"

"Yes."

Acton's eyes shot wide. "You have? Who?"

"You'll have to wait until you get here. I'll see you soon, my friend."

The call ended and Acton placed the phone on the table. "He says they've figured out who's buried at the necropolis."

Laura drew a quick breath. "Who?"

"The bastard wouldn't tell me. He said we'd have to wait until we got there."

"Where is there?" asked Tommy.

"Greece. Phaleron Delta, to be exact. It's a suburb of Athens. A few years ago, when they were excavating to build a new opera house and library, they discovered a massive burial mound. The site I think is over ten acres, and they've found over a thousand bodies so far. But there was one section they just recently excavated that has them puzzled. They found about eighty bodies, most lined up neatly, and shackled together, along with another smaller group that were shackled, but all mixed together as if just piled on top of each other. Most of the skeletons showed evidence of violent deaths, which suggested they were criminals, but for them to have been buried with at least a modicum of respect, suggested otherwise. It's a puzzle, and it would appear that our good professor might have discovered the solution."

"Sounds exciting!" gushed Mai.

"It does." Acton regarded Mai for a moment. Since they had received word that Laura couldn't have children due to a gunshot wound, they had both resigned themselves to growing old alone. But with Mai so young, Acton had come to almost think of her as a daughter, and was certain he was a father figure to her. A smile spread. "Why don't you two come with us? You may never get another chance to see something like this."

Laura squeezed his leg in approval.

And Mai's brightening face filled his heart with the warmth a father would at seeing his daughter so excited. "Could we?"

"Absolutely." He turned to Tommy. "Do you think you can get a few days off?"

"Umm, I sort of work for you, don't I?"

Acton grinned. "Oh yeah." He shrugged. "We'll take pictures for you."

Tommy's jaw dropped and Acton roared with laughter, Laura joining in, Mai taking a few moments before she realized it was all a joke. Tommy remained red-faced. "You're an evil man, Professor."

Laura laughed. "You have no idea."

En route to the Acropolis

City of Athens

632 BC

"You fool, the Olympics are that way!"

Cylon stared at the man, no anger in his heart toward him, for he wasn't the first to have shouted such a sentiment at him and his followers.

The day wasn't going as he had envisioned.

Not at all.

It had started strong. Over one hundred of his aristocratic friends had met at his home, all in their impressive armor, all filled with the righteous fervor such an occasion warranted. He had been a bundle of nerves himself, but all smiles, for today was to be a great day, and by the end of it, he would be Cylon, Tyrant of Athens.

Though to succeed, he needed the people behind him.

And all indications suggested they weren't.

At first, as they marched through the streets, his followers spreading the word, they were joined by dozens then hundreds. Yet when challenged, many of those who followed proved to be spectators rather than supporters, and broke away from his group, or continued to follow, joining in on the mocking or outright challenges, demanding by what right he thought he should rule Athens.

Then the guards appeared. They didn't interfere, they merely followed. As word spread throughout the city, and more of the authorities' security forces appeared, and the support they were counting on didn't solidify, he knew he was going to fail.

But failure wasn't an option.

He and the others had openly defied the archons, and treason such as this warranted death, no matter his position. He, due to his name, and the power of his father-in-law, might survive the day, but his supporters? They would surely die.

It made no sense.

The prophecy had been clear. He was to take power.

Yet that wasn't to be.

What had she said?

"Your family is one of honor, you are a hero of the people, and should you act wisely, you will succeed in unifying the people of Athens."

Didn't that mean he was to take power? How could it be interpreted any other way? Yet as he looked around him, the excitement and confidence of his followers wiped away, it appeared that the people of Athens were united against him.

"You will succeed in unifying the people of Athens."

Had he fallen into the trap so often set by Pythia and others like her? Had he been so blinded by his ambition, that he had seen the answer he had wanted in her words, ignoring the other possible interpretations?

Her words suggested that unity would only occur if he acted wisely, and he was rapidly becoming convinced that he hadn't. Basileios had been right. They should have waited. Three weeks would have given them time to organize, to build support. But two days? Clearly it hadn't been enough.

He had been a fool.

In his arrogance, he was certain the day honoring the great Zeus was the opening of the Olympics, because he had been so self-absorbed that he was convinced the gods were taking him into account in their plans for the people of Athens.

"I am an arrogant fool."

Basileios looked at him. "Why do you say that?"

"Look at the people. We have failed."

Basileios frowned, unable to deny the truth that surrounded them, no matter how much Cylon was certain his friend wanted to. "What are we going to do?"

"They'll execute us all, for sure."

"Or worse. I'd rather die with a blade to my stomach, than to spend a day in their prisons."

Cylon nodded. "True, but I wonder if there's a way for us to avoid both."

Basileios shook his head. "I can't imagine how."

Cylon rubbed between his thumb and forefinger the amulet given him by the high priestess, closing his eyes as they continued down the cobblestone street. The jeers outnumbered the shouts of support at least two-to-one, an optimistic estimate at best. Now, all he sought was a way out of this for his friends, for those who had committed themselves to this foolish venture.

Athena!

Surely, she would grant them protection, and her temple was sacred and nearby. The archons wouldn't dare touch them if they were under her protection. It would give them time for things to settle down, for cooler heads to prevail, and perhaps for a negotiated peace that would spare the others. And should it become necessary, he would sacrifice himself to save his friends without hesitation.

"To the Temple of Athena!"

He thrust his sword high in the air and broke out into a jog, his supporters following, the crowd parting for them, none willing to challenge the armed warriors.

"I take it you have a plan?"

He glanced over at Basileios. "We've lost the day. All that we can hope for now is to survive."

"A lofty goal. Might I inquire as to how you think you'll manage it?"

Cylon laughed. "We'll seek shelter in the temple. While there, the archons will try to negotiate our surrender. I will offer my life in exchange for the rest of you."

Basileios frowned. "Your plan is wise, in that they won't dare shed blood on holy ground. But it is foolish if you think any of us will agree to you sacrificing yourself for us."

Cylon slowed slightly. "If there was one person whose support I thought I could count on, it was you."

"You will always have my support. But don't think for a minute I will allow you to sacrifice yourself for me. *You* must survive the day, so that you can fight again. Athens needs you, even if these fools don't realize it. Athens doesn't need me. There are hundreds that will take my place."

"I can think of none who could replace my friend."

Basileios smiled. "Don't make me weep on an occasion such as this. I have a reputation to protect."

Cylon tossed his head back, laughing. "I hate to tell you this, on what might be our last day alive, but your free-flowing tears are a secret to no one."

Basileios' eyes narrowed. "I wonder who told them?"

"Perhaps the countless women you have used those tears on to win their hearts?"

Basileios frowned. "Perhaps that wasn't so wise."

Cylon pointed ahead, the temple now in sight. "We're almost there! Everyone inside! They can't touch us on holy ground!"

His supporters broke into a sprint, the panic they were feeling now evident. He had failed them, and he had failed Apollo.

He had interpreted Pythia's prophecy incorrectly.

And now her words he had ignored echoed in his head.

"To not heed this warning will result in a tragedy that will haunt you until the day you depart this plane of existence, and journey on to the next."

Thankfully, that day was likely today, and he wouldn't suffer long the tragedy about to befall him and his closest friends.

Outside Riyadh, Kingdom of Saudi Arabia
Present Day

"There's something I want. An artifact that came onto the market just last night."

Alexie Tankov glanced over his shoulder at Sheik Khalid bin Al Jabar, sitting in his gold and bejeweled throne in the center of the room, the platform able to rotate as desired to take in the spectacle that surrounded them—the actual fabled Amber Room, thought lost near the end of World War Two, but found by two annoyingly persistent archaeologists only months ago.

And liberated by his team.

For a substantial profit.

He had to admit, seeing it now for only the second time assembled, it was impressive. Gaudy to no end, but impressive. Some estimates had its worth at nearly half a billion dollars, though that meant little to men like the sheik. They wanted it for the prestige, not the value.

Tankov had little doubt that this room had been shared with a select few to elicit envy, and provoke admiration and respect.

It was the type of existence most could never imagine, where one had so much money, it could be thrown around by the hundreds of millions without even a second thought let alone a first.

It was a world that had made him and his team of former Russian Spetsnaz Special Forces operatives very rich.

Though with a price that he was no longer so comfortable living with.

The blood of innocents on his hands.

He returned his attention to the intricacies of the walls surrounding them. "And what is this artifact?"

"Something that belonged to Cylon himself."

Tankov's eyebrows narrowed slightly. "Never heard of him."

"He was involved in one of the first recorded events in Greek history. He attempted the violent takeover of Athens."

This caught Tankov's attention, and he turned toward Sheik Khalid. "Sounds like an interesting man."

"He was. And from what I've heard about this artifact, it is something I must have."

Tankov waved a hand at the half-billion-dollar room. "Don't you have enough?"

Khalid smiled. "The world isn't enough."

A James Bond theme played through Tankov's head as he wondered if the man in front of him had any idea that he had just quoted the family motto of the Bond clan. "For some people, I suppose. You know my fee. Where is it?"

"In Greece, a suburb of Athens. In your dossier, there will be a recording of a conversation between my contact and the person on the inside. She explains everything."

Tankov's eyebrows rose. "She?"

"Yes, she. This troubles you?"

Tankov shrugged. "I've met a lot of bad women in my time. One more means nothing to me."

"Good. As I was saying, she explains everything. The item is extremely valuable."

"Why? Is it made of gold or something?" He gestured at the room surrounding them. "Hardly something you need more of."

Khalid laughed. "No, it's a mystery."

"In what way?"

"Nobody knows what's inside it."

Tankov's eyes narrowed. "So, it's some sort of container?"

"Yes."

Tankov's eyes narrowed further. "Then why don't they just open it?"

Khalid shook his head. "They can't. They just found it, and they're waiting for the funding to do it properly."

Tankov frowned. "And you have the equipment to safely open it?"

Khalid's eyes shot wide. "I'd never open it!"

"Then why get it?"

"Just to have it. The mystery is the fun of it."

Tankov sighed. "You people and your oil money. It's ridiculous."

Khalid shrugged. "I've known no other life, so I have nothing to compare it to. I do highly recommend it, however." He leaned forward in his throne, his mouth curling into a smile. "And I've paid you quite handsomely over the years, enough to know that you too are very rich."

Tankov grunted. "I am."

"Exactly. Yet here you stand, criticizing me, while taking on yet another job for me, that will make you even richer. Why? Why keep working?"

Tankov chuckled. The man had him there. He was rich. Approaching nine figures rich. And so were his men. Though he was in charge, the rule was that anyone who survived split the payday evenly. That way everyone did what they were best at, rather than jockeying for a part of the job that would get a greater share.

It wouldn't do to have some of his team driving Porsches while others rode Peugeots.

He regarded the sheik. "For the thrill, I guess."

"Exactly. You get your thrills by stealing things. I get mine by possessing things. Like this room."

"So, you want this artifact. Why not just buy it if they've got someone on the inside?"

"I did, but she can't get it out without being caught. We need to go in and take it. She'll tell us when and where."

Tankov felt something in the pit of his stomach, and when he did, it almost always meant things were about to get difficult. "Where exactly is this?"

"At the Phaleron Delta Necropolis."

His head bobbed. "I've heard of it. It's a large site. I'm assuming it's guarded."

"Of course, though not heavily. You might have to kill some guards, though probably not many."

Tankov frowned. "I don't want any innocent people being killed."

Khalid's eyes narrowed as he stared at him. "You never had a problem doing it before." He gestured at the room. "In fact, you didn't when you stole this for me."

Tankov sighed. "Yes, and we went too far. I've changed my perspective on things. In the end, we succeeded, and we could have done so without the violence, or at least the killing."

"So you say."

"Yes, so I say. I don't mind killing bad people, but I'm not going to kill some poor son of a bitch just because he was there, doing his job."

Khalid regarded him, tapping his chin. "A thief with a conscience. How quaint."

"My team is good at what we do. The best. We can get your artifact without anybody getting killed." He stepped closer to the sheik. "Do we have the job?"

Khalid stared at him for what felt like minutes, then shook his head, leaning back in his throne. "No, I don't think so. This new philosophy you have disturbs me. It makes me think you might turn completely, and perhaps reveal who your clients are to the wrong people."

Tankov's chest tightened. "There's no chance of that. We'd be going to prison for life for what we've done. There are no deals for ex-Russian Special Forces."

"Still, I think our business is done. I need a team that doesn't have the scruples you now appear to."

Tankov bowed slightly. "That is your choice. I guess we'll part ways."

"I guess so. But be careful about making any hasty decisions. Not doing business with me means not doing business with any of my, shall we say, friends. You would effectively be out of business."

Tankov smiled. "When the others you hire botch the job and create too much heat, you'll be calling me."

"What makes you think they won't succeed?"

"There are not a lot of people who do what I do, and I already know you've been talking to the Suqut Brigade. You are aware they are an offshoot of ISIS? That they help steal and sell plundered artifacts to finance the cause?"

"I am."

"Then you are aware that they have no boundaries, and people like that leave messes that result in questions, and those lead to answers that might include this little oasis you've built yourself."

Khalid stared at him, his face devoid of emotion. "As I said, our business is concluded."

Tankov nodded. "Very well. As a courtesy, you will never be mentioned again. I expect the same shown to me and my team."

"That goes without saying."

Tankov leaned in closer. "And I'll give you one piece of unsolicited advice. Whatever you do, don't bring your new business partners here."

"Why?"

"These are dangerous men, who take what they want, and don't care who they kill to get it. They just might take a liking to this room, and are the types of barbarians who would just melt it down for the gold and amber, destroying a piece of history, which is something neither of us want."

Khalid's head bobbed slowly. "Sage advice. I shall be sure not to ignore it."

Tankov bowed. "It's been a pleasure."

"Likewise."

Tankov left the room, wondering how many days it would be before he heard from the sheik, begging him to sort out the mess created by his new partners.

Perhaps it might be best to plan ahead.

Temple of Athena, The Acropolis
City of Athens
632 BC

"Cylon, the archons are here!"

Cylon, huddled with the others around the statue of Athena, glanced over his shoulder to see one of his supporters pointing beyond the columns surrounding them. He recognized the leaders of the city as they clustered in a group, no doubt assessing the situation.

A situation not in his favor.

There were hundreds gathered, surrounding the temple, perhaps even a thousand. Yet most were there out of what he now assumed was morbid curiosity. They weren't here to support him, but instead to see what would happen to him and his followers.

Exactly what he had been discussing moments ago.

They needed an exit strategy.

Though most were aristocrats, the masses wouldn't recognize them, yet the archons would. At least most of them. It was too late for them to slip away and claim ignorance later if questioned. He had urged them to go home, but they had all to a one steadfastly refused.

He loved them for it.

And damned himself for their loyalty, for it would cost them their lives should things go poorly.

He smiled, deciding to test the resolve of the clearly worried archons. He approached Archon Eponymous Megacles, the senior of the group.

"Have you come to support us, Megacles?"

A broad smile spread across Megacles' face. He gestured at the sparse crowd. "If I have, then I am one of but a few."

"We had little time to organize a following, but it will come in time. Pythia herself said it was my duty to take control and save our great city."

Megacles frowned. "Knowing Pythia, she no doubt said something that could be interpreted in multiple ways. Surely, if you had interpreted her words correctly, you wouldn't be seeking sanctuary in the Temple of Athena, surrounded by our guards."

Cylon suppressed his own frown, for Megacles was correct. He was certain of it now. He should have waited for the Festival of Pandia, not the opening of the Olympics. It would have given them the time to garner a following, a following that would be with them now, their numbers too large to resist.

He regarded Megacles and the other archons. "I take it then that you will not support us?"

Megacles shook his head. "How can we, when not even the people follow you?"

"That will come."

"Perhaps, but until it does, Athens would be weakened, and made vulnerable. It may even fall into factions, a civil war breaking out that could leave us defenseless against outside invaders." Megacles sighed. "I'm afraid, my friend, your attempt to become tyrant has already failed. It is time for you to acknowledge the fact, lay down your arms, and accept your fate."

"And what fate might that be?"

"For these treasonous acts, there can be only one punishment."

Cylon nodded slowly, glancing over his shoulder at his friends, all standing silently within the temple walls, awaiting word, their expression a mix of hope, fear, and resignation. He turned to Megacles. "Would you see it in your hearts to forgive those who have foolishly followed me? To allow me to accept the punishment for all?"

Megacles shook his head. "I'm afraid the time has passed for mercies such as what you ask."

Cylon tensed as his strength threatened to leave him, then a spark of anger flared and he sucked in a deep breath, swelling his chest. "If your offer is for us all to die, then you leave me no choice. We will remain in the temple, under the goddess Athena's protection, and as we do so, word will spread of our plight, and our mission, and our supporters will increase in number." He leaned closer to the much smaller man.

"Before this day is out, I, Cylon, will rule Athens, and lead it into a bright new future!"

Megacles shrank away from him, though the fear was fleeting, for the reality of the situation left it unwarranted. He stared at Cylon with what appeared to be genuine sympathy and regret. "I fear, my friend, that before this day is out, you will be dead, along with all those who follow you."

Athens International Airport

Spata, Greece

Present Day

Acton waved from the top of the steps of their private jet, a Gulf V that was part of a lease-share network that Laura had been a member of for years. Her wealth was staggering, much of it inherited upon the death of her brother, an Internet tycoon who had sold while the getting was good. The rest came from the wise stewardship of her windfall and their reasonable lifestyle.

There were no mansions in their life, no fancy cars beyond the Porsche she had inherited.

But there was always first-class travel and a lot of it, good food and drink, and generosity shown to their friends and family, as well as their students.

None of their students would be left behind for lack of family money on their digs—anonymous donations always arrived just in time.

As he descended the steps, he looked for Antoniou's constant companion, Juno, but didn't see her.

"My friends, welcome, welcome!" Antoniou held out his arms and Acton joined him in an exuberant embrace and double-cheek kiss. "I trust your flight was good?" He eyed the jet. "I suppose it must have been."

Acton laughed. "It was. As you can see, I married well."

"Indeed!" Antoniou shook Laura's hand. "Professor Palmer, it is indeed an honor."

Laura smiled. "Laura, please." She turned, holding out a hand toward Tommy and Mai. "May I present Mr. Tommy Granger and Miss Mai Trinh, both graduate students at James' university."

Antoniou shook their hands. "A pleasure."

Acton gave Mai a wink. "I hope you don't mind we brought them, but without our servants, life is just unbearable."

Antoniou stared at him for a moment, then at the two youngsters. "I, umm, I…"

Acton burst out laughing, slapping the man on his back. "You should see your face, my friend. I'm just kidding of course. Now, where is Juno? I don't think I've ever seen the two of you apart."

"You'll see her soon." Antoniou urged them toward the waiting SUV, and they all climbed in, Acton in the passenger seat. Antoniou held up his left hand, revealing a wedding band. "You should know that she is now my wife."

Acton grinned. "I had a suspicion there was something there. The way she looked at you was always with total devotion. I knew she loved you five years ago."

Antoniou sighed as he started the engine. "It took me a little longer to realize the truth, and once I did, I realized I loved her too. The age difference is a little ridiculous, twenty years, but I'm nearly sixty now, she's almost forty. Kids are behind us both, and, well, it just made sense. We finally realized we were both lonely souls who were spending almost every waking hour together, and happy doing so. Why not every sleeping hour as well?"

Tommy offered up a fist bump. "Professor!"

The women in the car glared at him, Acton giving him a bemused expression, the fist slowly lowering.

Antoniou stared at the young man for a moment, not sure what to do, then smiled, bumping the fist. "You're right, I *am* a lucky man!" He returned his attention to the road. "I can't wait for you to see her. I know she's looking forward to seeing you again, Jim, and is eager to meet you as well, Professor—sorry, Laura."

"I'm looking forward to it as well." Laura placed a hand on Tommy's still extended arm, forcing it back into his lap. His chin dropped onto his chest as his cheeks flushed.

"Listen, I have a confession to make."

Everyone turned toward Antoniou, including the butterflies forming in Acton's stomach. "I don't think I like the sound of that."

"It's nothing serious, nothing dangerous, but I don't know who I can trust."

Acton exchanged a concerned glance with Laura. "I *really* don't like the sound of that. How about you stop teasing it out, and just tell us everything."

Antoniou nodded, inhaling deeply. "You're right, of course. There have been a series of thefts at the dig site. Minor items, but historically significant nonetheless. We are talking items that are thousands of years old, many of them remarkably preserved."

"Do you know who's behind it?"

Antoniou shook his head. "No. It's a massive dig site, as you know, but due to budget limitations, we're concentrating on the recent discovery we made."

"The chained together bodies."

"Yes. We have a few guards, but they are spread thin, and other than the odd supplier that delivers us things, it is mostly government personnel and grad students from our university. And even then, we're talking barely a few dozen people." He sighed. "Oh, to have the money we used to have. My friend, Greece is a very different place today. We were foolish, trying to be a socialist state in a capitalist world. Can you believe how few people paid their taxes?" He shook his head. "We were idiots, and now we're paying the price, and will be for at least a generation."

Acton felt sorry for the man. Antoniou was a hard worker, certainly not one of the freeloaders that some of the Greek population had become, and now because of those people, his life's work was suffering.

When people were asked to sacrifice so much to get back on track, there was little tolerance for money going to the sciences, especially archaeology, where something could simply be sealed back up and looked at in another decade or two, when the money was flowing again.

But this discovery was too important to be left unstudied, and now that the world knew it existed, thieves would descend upon it should it be left for another day.

Perhaps we can help with a small donation.

"So why do you need us?"

"I need people I can trust, even if only for a few days. Juno and I are exhausted. We've been taking shifts, staying at the site every hour of every day, at least one of us, and we're reaching our breaking point. And despite this, items continue to disappear." He sighed, shaking his head. "I'm sorry for getting you here under false pretenses, my friend, but would you have come if I told you the truth?"

Tommy grunted. "Knowing these two, they probably would have been here quicker."

Acton laughed, leaning back and giving Tommy a gentle punch to the shoulder as the others joined in. "Too true! Too true!" He turned back to Antoniou. "If things are so dire, perhaps we should go there right away."

Antoniou brightened at the suggestion. "Would you mind? I hated leaving her alone there." He frowned. "Something is wrong, I know it, and I just don't know who I can trust besides her, and those in this vehicle."

Acton patted him on the shoulder. "Then get a little heavy on that pedal."

Antoniou glanced at him as the car accelerated. "I didn't want to scare anyone."

Acton laughed. "We've all driven with Laura. Trust me, there's nothing you can do that could scare us."

Antoniou proved him wrong.

Temple of Athena, The Acropolis

City of Athens

632 BC

Cylon frowned as the sun faded, torches beginning to light around their sanctuary. "At least I was right about more coming."

Basileios nodded, apparently choosing to ignore Cylon's tone. "True, and some of them are even here to support us. If we can hold out long enough, we still might win. I know some of those that are here. I've been watching. They are working the crowd, and have been winning some of them over."

Cylon resisted the temptation to give in to the hope Basileios was suggesting existed. It was too late. More guards now surrounded them, and even soldiers belonging to some of the other aristocratic families had arrived, and were definitely not there to support him.

This was a lost cause.

And he didn't know what to do.

He had already been told that they all faced death for their actions. He couldn't care less if he were put to death, but it tormented him terribly to think the others would suffer the same fate.

It wasn't fair.

It wasn't reasonable.

"Give me a moment."

Cylon strode from the safety their sanctuary provided, and approached the archons, now joined by several heads of the aristocratic families. He exchanged greetings with them, then turned his attention to Megacles.

"Are you still steadfast in your resolve to see us all dead?"

Cylon enjoyed the uncomfortable reaction from Megacles as the new arrivals stared at him in shock, evidently not aware of the sentence already pronounced upon those who would dare rebel.

"Is this true, Megacles? Have you already sentenced these people to death?"

And with that one indignant question from Lykos, a man Cylon respected tremendously, he knew he had just bought his people a chance at life.

"Well, I, umm, was merely interpreting the law as I understood it."

Lykos growled. "The law should not be absolute. It should allow for some flexibility. Has anyone died here today?"

Megacles shook his head. "No, but only for the fact no one supported Cylon and his people."

"How can you know that? Are you a seer who can see what might have been? Are you the next high priestess of Delphi?"

Snickers surrounded them, a slight smile escaping Cylon's tight control of his emotions.

"You insult me, sir."

"And you insult us all by proclaiming judgment upon these people before hearing their case." Lykos shook his head, turning to Cylon. "Cylon, my boy, I cannot condone what you have done here today. I fear my house would have opposed your attempt at power. But I know charismatic men, and the affect they can have on weaker minds, and you, my boy, are one of the most charismatic men I have ever known. Those that support you should not be put to death for following you. Yes, they should be punished, harshly perhaps, but not slaughtered for falling sway to the words of a man such as yourself." He stepped closer. "Are you willing to die for your actions here today?"

Cylon's stomach flipped as he realized he was about to be given the out he so desperately wanted for his people. "I am."

"And you are willing to accept full responsibility for the actions of all those you hold sway to?"

Cylon's chest swelled as he squared his shoulders. "I am."

Lykos patted him on the arm. "As I suspected you would." He turned to the archons. "I think then we have our solution. Cylon and his followers will surrender, accompany us to the court for trial, and he will accept full responsibility for the events of this troubling day. In exchange for his life, the others will serve a sentence acceptable to the court, that does not include death."

"Or banishment."

Lykos glanced at Cylon, then nodded. "Or banishment. We want these people to return to their former positions of honor, having been shown that the current leadership of our great city is both merciful and wise, and not in need of violent replacement." Lykos paused, looking about at the others. "Are we all agreed?"

Heads bobbed, though Megacles' remained frozen in place, long enough that Cylon feared he might scuttle the entire deal.

Then he sighed audibly. "Very well."

Cylon smiled, extending a hand. "I thank you, Archon Eponymous Megacles. It is clear that I was mistaken in my belief that you and your fellow archons should be, shall we say, replaced."

Megacles chuckled, taking the hand. "I wonder if the roles were reversed, would you be showing me the mercy I now show you."

Cylon squeezed the hand slightly tighter. "Fortunately, we will never know."

Phaleron Delta Necropolis
Athens, Greece
Present Day

Acton was giddy and tense at the same time. The excitement of seeing the massive necropolis, combined with his concerns over the thefts, had him a bundle of nerves. It was bad enough they almost always got themselves into trouble when they ventured outside their home, it was worse knowing there already was a problem.

Minor thefts. Nothing to worry about.

And he might have believed that if it weren't for the expression creasing Professor Juno Galanos' face as she exchanged a hug with her husband. Acton shook her hand.

"Juno, it's so good to see you again. I understand congratulations are in order."

She smiled weakly. "Yes, and to you as well."

Antoniou stared at his wife with concern. "You seem troubled, my love."

She threw up her hands, shaking her head. "I'm so sorry. I'm a terrible host, but we just discovered another artifact missing."

A loud, long sigh escaped from Antoniou. "What now?"

"A pair of shackles."

Antoniou cursed. "That's the third pair now, isn't it?"

She nodded. "And if we don't find out who's behind this, it won't be the last." She lowered her voice. "If we don't get a handle on this soon, we'll lose control of the site."

Antoniou shook his head. "If we let the government run this operation, it will be a fiasco."

Acton surveyed the area. "I thought this was being managed by the government already?"

"It is, on paper. They oversee everything officially, and manage the budget, what little of it there is. But the actual scientific work is being managed by us through the university."

"But if we can't keep what we discover from being stolen, they'll take that over too." Juno pulled at her short hair. "I don't know what to do about it."

Laura gestured toward the front gate they had passed through moments ago. "You have guards. How are they getting past?"

A burst of air erupted from Juno's mouth. "They're useless. Minimum wage, no weapons. They don't care. Besides, there are too few of them to cover an area this large. And they're always taking small items. Unless we're willing to have full body searches, and vehicles torn apart at the end of every day, there's no way to stop them. We just don't have the manpower."

Acton frowned. "Could the guards be behind it?"

She shook her head. "No, I don't think so. We don't let them into the site itself. Their job is to guard the perimeter." She lowered her voice. "I think it's someone on the inside. It has to be."

Antoniou put an arm around his wife's shoulders. "I fear my wife is right, and it makes me sick to my stomach to think that someone, an academic, could be behind these thefts, but…"

"Can you hire more guards?" asked Mai.

"Or concentrate them all at the gate at the end of the day for the searches you were mentioning?" suggested Tommy.

Juno shook her head. "No, we just don't have the budget, and if we repositioned the guards, anyone could just toss something over the fence and pick it up later."

"Surely the government could free up some funds to protect such an important site."

Antoniou appeared embarrassed as he replied to Laura. "We, umm, haven't told them."

Acton nodded. "Because you're afraid they'll take over."

"Exactly. Things are bad in Greece, and have been for years. There simply isn't any money to spare. I fear they'll close us down completely and wait for more money. We've held them off for now, and as long as we keep producing, and publishing, I think we'll be fine. But if word got out about these thefts? We'd be finished."

"What about private donations?" asked Laura, Acton giving her a slight smile, knowing where this was heading.

"We are receiving some, just enough to keep us with supplies and students when the funding falls short, but it's not enough, not for large items like security."

"Perhaps we can help."

Antoniou stared at her, aghast. "Absolutely not! I invited you here for advice, not for money."

Laura laughed. "Don't give it a second thought. We could help fund your dig until the government comes through."

Antoniou shook his head. "No, we're making do. It's just this security issue that's the real problem. We don't know how to deal with it."

Laura smiled. "Well, it just so happens I know someone."

Temple of Athena, The Acropolis
City of Athens
632 BC

"This is insanity."

Cylon smiled gently at Basileios. "No, it is reality. We're not getting the support of the people, as we had hoped." He patted his friend on the shoulder. "You were right. I misinterpreted the prophecy, and in my own arrogance, acted too soon. But only *I* should pay for that mistake, not you. The archons have agreed that only I shall die for what occurred here today. You will all be punished, but you will survive, and will not be banished. Lykos himself said you should return to your former positions." He stared at those surrounding him. "It is a good compromise. Better than any of us could have expected."

Reluctant nods finally appeared from his friends, but Basileios was having none of it. "Nonsense. We were all willing to die, and I for one still am. And do you truly trust Megacles? He's one of the prime reasons we decided to take action. The moment we leave these walls, the moment we are no longer under the protection of our goddess, he will order his men to strike." He shook his head vehemently. "No, *you* must survive. You are our leader, and there is no doubt the Oracle meant that you were to lead the people. Our only mistake was on what day to act, not whether or not we *should* act. You are destined to lead Athens, though perhaps not today. And if it is to be another day, then you must survive to see it."

Cylon stared at his friend. "What are you saying? That I break the deal I just made and abandon you all like a coward?"

Basileios shook his head. "No, it is only abandonment if you do so against *our* will. We want you to save yourself. Let us provide you with a diversion so that you can escape, so that you can live on to fight another day. Athens needs you, but it doesn't need us. Let us be the distraction that saves you, and perhaps, Apollo willing, we too will survive to fight at your side."

Cylon's eyes burned and his chest ached at the words of his friend, and even more so at the unanimous agreement expressed by the others, scores of arms reaching out toward him in solidarity.

Yet he couldn't let them die.

"There has to be another way," he finally managed, thankful his voice didn't crack with emotion. "If they discover that I am not with you, they will surely kill you."

Basileios smiled as a thought apparently occurred to him. He stared up at the statue of Athena towering over them. "Not if we remain under her protection."

Lower Nubia, Egypt

Present Day

Retired Special Air Services Lieutenant Colonel Cameron Leather lay in his hammock, a tan fedora covering his face as he enjoyed the gentle breeze that took the edge off the desert heat. Most of the camp was quiet now, the afternoons in the Egyptian desert too hot for work on days like today.

It suited him fine.

He didn't mind the heat too much. It was dry, allowing his perspiration to evaporate and cool his body, and relief wasn't far, Professor Laura Palmer's tent equipped with air conditioning. All were welcome to take the edge off at any time under her watch.

When she was away, which was most of the time now, her two recently married senior grad students, Terrence and Jenny Mitchell, were in charge, and now occupied the tent. They weren't as qualified, obviously, but they were proving more competent than he had feared they might be. Terrence was hilariously awkward, especially during combat training.

When Acton and Laura began to have some problems with outside "organizations," she had requested he and his men train them in self-defense. That had expanded over the years to include her students if they wanted to participate, and privately had extended into Special Forces levels of training. He had taught them hand-to-hand combat, weapons including guns and knives, explosives, surveillance techniques, and more. Anything he could think of they might need, or anything they found they lacked after yet another incident.

It was always interesting.

Terrence had proven his bravery on several occasions, which had been stunning to behold each time, and it might explain how he had managed to land Jenny, a girl way out of his league.

Opposites attract.

Acton and Laura were a perfect match. They were so much alike, he sometimes swore they were twins separated at birth. Theirs was the type of relationship he wanted. His marriage had been an unmitigated disaster, and had ended long ago. They wanted completely different things. He wanted a career in the military, serving his country, and she wanted a banker to satisfy her expensive tastes.

He had resigned himself to stress relievers, but on a recent trip into Cairo, he had met someone.

Someone spectacular.

Someone that terrified him.

Because he could actually see a future there, after just one wild weekend.

Adelaide Burnett.

She worked at the Australian embassy, mid-thirties, long curly blond hair, and bronzed skin.

And a bundle of energy.

Adelaide had kept him on his toes the entire three days they were together. An old Aussie SAS buddy had called him after being assigned as private security to the embassy, and Leather had met him for drinks. She was with the group, introductions were made, and after too many shots and a few dares, they were inseparable for the duration of his leave.

She had made him feel like a teenager, and he had been reminded of what those butterflies felt like.

It was good.

And genuinely terrifying.

And he couldn't wait to see her tomorrow.

He had two days off, and he didn't plan to see a sliver of sunlight the entire time.

Something twitched.

He sighed.

Life is good.

The satellite phone sitting on his chest rang, spoiling his mood. "Go for Leather."

"You sound like you're in a good mood."

He smiled at his client's voice. He liked Laura. She was a good sort, friendly though demanding in a reasonable way. Her wants and needs made sense, and usually were in line with his way of thinking.

And she had unlimited resources, unlike many of his previous clients who argued over the pennies.

"I am. I have two days off starting tomorrow."

"Oh no! I forgot about that."

He could sense something in her voice, and he rolled out of the hammock, heading for his tent. "What's wrong? Are you in danger?"

"No, no, nothing like that, though we do have a security issue that I thought you might be able to help with."

He stepped inside his tent and took a seat at the small table to the left of the entrance. "Tell me everything."

What he heard had him breathing easy after only a few moments. Stolen minor artifacts were only a threat to his client if she interrupted the thief in progress, and while a concern, he had a feeling this was a petty criminal as opposed to an organized ring that might carry serious weapons.

But it was still a risk, and the thefts, irrespective of danger to his client, had to be stopped.

"I think it's better if I contract this out."

"I understand. You've got your leave, and you should take it."

He chuckled, a smile spreading.

She is the best *client.*

"No, that's not what I meant. I have an old colleague, Greek, who has a private security firm. They already have all the necessary permits to operate on Greek soil, armed. My team would need to get permits if we wanted to carry weapons, and it could take months. I'll give him a shout and see if he can send a team there to help with security."

"That would be wonderful, Cameron, thank you."

"I'll make arrangements to join you as soon as possible. I was heading to Cairo regardless, so should be able to catch a flight in short order. It's just a hop to Athens from there."

"No, no, you had plans, I'm sure. Take your vacation. I've been working you too hard. How about you send one of your men?"

He thought of Adelaide and what he had planned for her and closed his eyes, picturing her naked form on top of him.

Oh, what I sacrifice for the job.

"No, none of them have served with my friend. It's best that I'm there since he can be a little rough around the edges."

"You sound disappointed. I feel terrible."

He frowned, not realizing he had failed to keep his tone neutral. "It's nothing."

"It's a girl, isn't it?"

He chuckled. "Ma'am, I think I've been working for you for too long."

She laughed. "I have a feeling you'll retire from this job, rather than move on to the next."

"I live to serve. Don't worry about her, she'll understand."

"Is she in Cairo?"

"Yes. She works at the Australian Embassy."

There was a pause. "I have a wonderful idea. Why don't you bring her?"

His eyebrows shot up. "Ma'am?"

"Bring her. I don't think this is a dangerous assignment. I think we just need to get some additional security set up, that should deter the thief, then we'll be out of here in a few days. Bring her, I'll set you guys up at our hotel in a suite, and when you're off duty, you two can enjoy each other's company."

The idea sounded fantastic, though he hated mixing business with pleasure. Any other assignment, he would have refused outright, but Laura was correct—this wasn't a dangerous assignment. This was just beefing up security at what was obviously an underfunded dig site. Adelaide wouldn't even be at the site, just the hotel and its surrounds. He would get to spend his evenings and nights with her, far better than the other prospect he was facing of no time together at all.

"I'll float the idea past her, see what she thinks."

"Wonderful! I'll arrange the hotel. Let me know when to expect your Greek friends."

"Will do."

He ended the call and leaned back in his chair, a smile on his face. He'd rather spend a few days in Athens than Cairo any day.

Though the inside of a hotel room is pretty much the same anywhere.

He grinned, dialing her number, hoping against hope she could leave the country on short notice.

Otherwise one of them would have to go AWOL.

Temple of Athena, The Acropolis
City of Athens
632 BC

Their demand hadn't taken long to be fulfilled, and now they had one impossibly long strand of thread, consisting of dozens of tied together spools provided by those who lived in the area and had heeded their plea. Basileios watched with pride and regret as his friend tied one end to the outstretched hand of their goddess Athena, who had protected them this entire time. Cylon stepped down and handed the other end to Basileios, then embraced him for what Basileios was certain was the last time.

"You have always been a good friend to me."

Basileios' voice cracked. "And you have been the best to me."

Cylon sighed. "I had always thought we would die in battle together. Never did I think I would be leaving you alone to fight, while I ran away like a coward."

Basileios gripped his friend's shoulder. "You are the bravest man I know, and no coward would willingly face what lies ahead for you. You are destined to lead, and you will, but without the help of your closest friends and advisors. Your path will be even more difficult than it was this morning, yet I know in my heart you will succeed."

Cylon smiled. "Then you have more confidence than me, my friend."

"It's time," hissed one of his men from the shadows, everyone having taken hold of a portion of the long thread.

Cylon nodded, removing from around his neck the amulet given him by Pythia. He pressed it into Basileios' hand. "Let it bring you the success it failed to bring me."

Basileios clasped it against his chest. "I shall treasure it." He gave his friend one last hug, his chest aching as if his heart were about to burst, then motioned to the four men assigned to give the best friend, and the greatest man he had ever known, any hope of escape.

As the torches inside the temple were doused to provide them with cover, Cylon stared at those gathered. "Should any of us not survive the night, then I shall see you again in Elysium, and there we shall rejoice together, with no regrets, over what we tried here this tragic day."

And with that, Cylon slipped into the darkness with his escort, and Basileios, tears streaming down his face, silently led those who remained from the temple that had protected them, and into the uncertainty that lay ahead.

Phaleron Delta Necropolis

Athens, Greece

Present Day

Basil Antoniou pointed at the long line of excavated skeletons, all in a neat row, all with their hands shackled together over their heads.

An unusual configuration.

Acton scratched his chin. "Do you have an explanation for this? This burial method?"

Antoniou looked at him, a slight smile on his face. "Why don't you give me your theory, Professor?"

Acton chuckled, taking the bait willingly. "*If* you insist." He stepped closer to the solemn sight. "The shackles suggest they were criminals, or at least prisoners. And were so when they died. There's no way they would be buried this way if they were innocent."

Antoniou nodded. "Agreed."

Laura stepped forward, kneeling beside the first body. "And these men were buried with respect." She gestured along the straight line. "They were all positioned neatly, orderly. If they were being discarded en masse as prisoners, they would likely have simply been tossed into a mass grave." She frowned, shaking her head. "Back then, the bodies of dead criminals were rarely treated with respect like this."

Antoniou smiled, his eyes widening suggestively. "Unless?"

Acton pursed his lips. "Unless they were nobility. Despite their crimes, they still would have been accorded respect. The authorities wouldn't have dared offend the families."

"Go on."

"According to what I read, they've been carbon dated to the third quarter of the seventh century BC."

"Yes. Confirmed multiple times."

"Which, according to incorrect news reports, places them between 650 and 675. But *we* know that the third quarter of the seventh century BC is actually the opposite of that, and places them between 625 and 650 BC."

Antoniou's head bobbed appreciatively. "I'm glad you picked up on that. You wouldn't believe how many deaf ears my pleas fell on to have those reports corrected. And once our discovery is announced, those erroneous reports will be used to try and debunk our theory."

Acton stared at the bodies, noting signs of wounds—chipped and broken bones, and head wounds that suggested impact by blunt objects, perhaps stones. "Well, I've always felt, from the moment that this find was announced, that there was only one possible explanation for this."

Antoniou smiled. "That these are those Plutarch referred to? That these are those who were massacred?"

Acton nodded. "Exactly. But other than the timing, and the fact the circumstances of their death seem to corroborate with Plutarch's account, no proof has been found." He paused, a smile creeping onto his face. "This discovery you keep alluding to. You've found the proof, haven't you?"

Antoniou put an arm around his wife's shoulders. "We have. And it proves it beyond any doubt."

Outside the Temple of Athena, The Acropolis

City of Athens

632 BC

Cylon hid behind the statue of Athena with the others as they stripped off their armor. It was dark inside the temple, the only light from the torches surrounding the outside, and as his followers slowly made their way out, all gripping the thread that would keep them linked to the goddess and the protection she provided, the attentions of those outside followed them.

It was working.

The torches outside moved, converging on the other side, leaving the opposite side almost devoid of people. Orders were shouted and the crowds parted, allowing his people passage unscathed.

He said a silent prayer to Apollo and the goddess Athena, then turned to his men. "Ready?"

They nodded as one.

"Then let's go. Quietly, calmly." He led the way, striding from their hiding position to one of the outer columns, then pressed against it, the others doing the same at columns on either side. He peered into the darkness and smiled.

Nobody remained, though there was still some torchlight from fixed positions.

He sheathed his sword, hiding it under his robes, then stepped casually out from behind the column, striding across the square and toward an alleyway closest their position.

Someone shouted to their right. "Some of them are escaping!"

His escort converged on his position and grabbed him by both arms, hauling him toward the alleyway as he at first struggled against them, wanting instead to fight at their side.

But if he did, they would all die, and they would have died for nothing.

He stopped resisting, and instead broke out into a sprint toward the narrow opening, his men releasing their grip as he was now committed to their bidding.

Swords clashed behind him as he reached the alleyway. More shouts and the pounding of footfalls echoed behind him. Someone cried out. It was one of their own, he was sure. He cringed as yet another was heard meeting his end.

He pressed forward, emerging from the alleyway and into another street. He sprinted in the opposite direction of his home, as there would be no safety found there, and instead headed toward the port and the security provided by the unfamiliar faces of those not from these parts.

And prayed for the souls of his fallen friends.

Phaleron Delta Necropolis

Athens, Greece

Present Day

Shouts from outside had Acton and the others heading for the ramp before Antoniou's major discovery could be revealed. There was no sense of urgency, just excitement, and as he emerged from the pit, he smiled in relief at the sight of two black SUVs quickly emptying of their occupants and cargo.

An imposing figure of a man strode toward them, decked out in gear fit for any well-equipped Special Ops soldier, and a casual salute was given.

"I am Darius Korba. Which one of you is Professor Palmer?"

Laura stepped forward, extending a hand. "I am. Are you Cameron's man?"

"Colonel Leather and I had the distinction of serving together, yes. He has briefed me on the situation, and we are fully prepared to take over security of the site."

Acton noticed Antoniou bristle at the words. "I think there might have been a slight misunderstanding. We need you to *supplement* the security, not take it over. This site is controlled by the Greek government, so we can't supplant their people without permission."

Korba bowed slightly. "Understood, sir. I presume you are Professor Acton?"

Acton nodded. "I am."

"Excellent. Colonel Leather has informed me that the two of you are well-trained. I may require your assistance later, until the rest of my team arrives tomorrow."

"You're bringing more?"

"This is just an advance team of six to get monitoring equipment set up. Another six are arriving tomorrow. That will give us enough to rotate shifts."

"Will twelve be enough?" asked Laura.

"From what I've been told, we are dealing with minor thefts, not a physical threat. If we were worried about some sort of attack in numbers, then we'd definitely want more men. We'll set up monitoring equipment to secure the perimeter. No one will be able to get in or out except at the main gate. That will be our chokepoint where we'll search anyone and anything leaving the premises. With the proper scanners and trained personnel, it shouldn't disrupt activities too much. If we don't find your thief, I think we'll at least bring a halt to their activities.

We'll train the staff here on how to use the equipment we've installed, and once you staff up with locals, we'll move on."

Acton was impressed. The man clearly had confidence, and appeared to know what he was talking about. Acton agreed with every word Korba had said. This was all to prevent a thief from continuing his or her crimes, not to protect against a terrorist attack.

And he also liked how the man spoke of training the in-place personnel, then moving on. He didn't sound like someone looking to establish a long-term foothold on the location, billing them through the nose for months or years.

Leather had chosen wisely.

Korba turned to Professor Antoniou. "Sir, are you Professor Antoniou?"

"I am."

Korba shook his hand, switching to Greek. The words flew fast and furious, Acton picking up a fair bit of it, though his forte was Ancient Greek, and his skillset there consisted of being able to read it, not understand it in rapid conversation.

Whatever was said seemed to please both Antoniou and his wife. More handshakes were exchanged, then Korba turned to Acton.

"Please excuse me. I have to see to my men. We'll meet again in one hour and I'll update you on our progress." He bowed his head at everyone, then spun on his heel, heading back to the SUVs and the piles of unloaded gear, snapping orders to his men.

Acton sighed, then turned to Antoniou. "Well, I have a feeling your security issue has just been taken care of."

76

Antoniou nodded, though didn't seem as confident. "Hopefully, but it still doesn't tell us who is behind the thefts in the first place."

"True. Perhaps it's time to call in the authorities."

Antoniou stared at him, aghast. "Oh no! We couldn't do that! Like I said, they'll shut us down. We need to figure it out ourselves, then deliver the guilty party into their hands. Only then can we prove we are good custodians of this find."

Acton didn't agree with the man, though it wasn't his place to say anything. He was a guest here, and this wasn't his country, though the discovery belonged to all the people of the world. Yes, the Greeks should be allowed to keep whatever was found on their soil, but it should be enjoyed as part of a worldwide collection of history.

All history, everywhere, should be respected, preserved, and enjoyed, by all mankind. This was why he was always enraged when he read reports or saw videos of groups like ISIS or the Taliban destroying irreplaceable history, of how the burning of thousands of priceless pieces of art by the Nazis gutted him.

These things were irreplaceable.

These things were who they all were.

This city, Athens, was where the very idea of democracy was born. If those initial cornerstones hadn't been laid so long ago, who knew what type of world they might live in now. The history that surrounded them was awe inspiring. There wasn't a street in Athens without a building on it older than the oldest European built structure in America.

He loved it here, and this site that they had been touring was one of the greatest finds ever made.

And it made him determined to save it, though how he could, without the cooperation of the man in charge, he wasn't sure.

Acton nodded at Antoniou, biting his tongue for now. "We'll do it your way, of course, my friend."

Antoniou breathed a sigh of relief. "Thank you, Jim, thank you." He smiled. "Now, how about I show you our greatest discovery to date. The discovery that proves who is actually buried here?"

The Acropolis
City of Athens
632 BC

Basileios' chest ached as he heard the fighting behind him, and there was no doubt their ruse had been discovered. He prayed his friend had managed to escape, and as the sounds of the fight dwindled with no shouts of victory, he smiled.

May Apollo and Athena protect you, my friend.

"What is the meaning of this trickery?"

Basileios wiped the smile off his face before turning toward Megacles. "To what trickery do you refer?"

Megacles glared at him. "You know exactly what I'm talking about. Some of your people tried to escape." He stared down the long line of supporters. "And where is Cylon? Shouldn't he be leading you criminals?"

Basileios shook his head. "No, he is bringing up the rear. He wanted to make sure everyone got out safely."

Megacles jabbed at the air between them. "If I find out he has broken our deal!"

Basileios shrugged. "I'm sure he's at the end of the line. Go see for yourself."

Megacles stormed off and Basileios didn't dare look at the others as he continued to lead them toward the court, the thread providing them the goddesses' protection still gripped tightly in his hand, several additional spools of thread stuffed in his robes should it not prove long enough. They didn't have far to go, and would be there soon. The fact they still had not heard word of Cylon's fate continued to give him hope that his friend had escaped.

But he feared their fate once Megacles discovered Cylon wasn't at the end of the line like he had said. Though he had said he was willing to die, he was hoping he would see his wife and children one last time before his fate was sealed by the betrayal he had orchestrated.

A roar of rage erupted from behind him, then Megacles' voice echoed through the street. "Where is Cylon?"

Worried utterances rippled down the line, and Basileios turned to the man behind him. "Keep going. Whatever you do, remain calm, and keep a hold of the thread. Athena will protect you."

The man nodded, fear in his eyes, but he took the lead as Basileios hurried toward the end of the line, making sure to always keep one alternating hand on the thread that he hoped was more than a symbolic link to the protections they needed Athena to afford them.

"Search the area!" shouted Megacles as Basileios approached. "I want him found!" Megacles glared at Basileios as he arrived, pointing a finger at him. "You would follow a coward that would abandon you? Does he realize what he has done?"

Basileios drew a long breath, thrusting his shoulders back and his chest out. "We happily sacrifice ourselves so that Cylon may live. And should he have escaped, then I pray that Pythia's prophesy will come true, and that one day he will lead our people to the greatness we risk losing."

Megacles growled. "None of you will see the rise of tomorrow's sun, let alone the day Cylon will rule."

Basileios held up the thread, the line still marching toward the justice they had been promised. "Remember, we are under the protection of the goddess Athena. This link to her, still strong despite being so delicate, is proof that she protects us, and expects your promise of our safe passage to be honored."

Megacles glared at him then drew his sword, sliding it across the exposed thread at the end of the line, slicing it in two, the severed ends gently fluttering to the ground.

Basileios and the others who witnessed the blasphemous act gasped in horror, and he gripped the amulet tightly in his hands as he realized their fate had just been sealed.

"Kill them all."

Phaleron Delta Necropolis

Athens, Greece

Present Day

"We only discovered this a few days ago. We haven't even told the Ministry yet. It far exceeds anything we have found to this point, and frankly, I doubt anything else we find here can rival it."

Acton clasped his hands behind his neck, desperate for Antoniou to get to the point, his heart hammering with excitement. But he had been in this position before—the big reveal—and he wasn't about to deprive his friend of this moment.

"You're killing us, Basil!" cried Laura, her fingers drumming rapidly on her stomach as she burned off the nervous energy.

Antoniou smiled, then with a flourish removed the cloth covering whatever it was he had been hiding.

Acton gasped and Laura cooed as they circled the table holding the priceless artifact. It was a jar, or more likely an urn considering their

82

location within a necropolis, perfectly preserved. Care had been taken to remove any dirt stuck to it, and the skill used was evident, as not a crack was to be seen.

Acton leaned in closer, examining the top. He pointed at the lid. "Sealed with wax?"

"Yes."

His heart skipped a beat as he exchanged an excited glance with Laura. "So, you don't know what's inside?"

"No idea. Except…"

Acton stopped, turning to Antoniou. "Except?"

"Except that there definitely is something inside."

Acton closed his eyes, imagining a thousand possibilities. "Any ideas?"

"None, except that it is small, and likely metal by the sounds it made scraping on the bottom of the jar when we gently rotated it."

Acton stood back, not trusting he wouldn't collapse in his excitement. He found a large stone and sat on it. "This is exciting. I don't know why, but it just is. I feel like a kid who wants to tear open the box of Cheerios to get to the prize inside."

Antoniou laughed. "You have no idea how hard it has been to resist opening this, right here, right now, but we're waiting for the proper facilities to be made available to have it scanned without disturbing the contents."

Acton nodded. "A wise precaution. When do you anticipate being able to open it?"

"Very soon. As early as next week. You are both welcome to join us, of course."

Laura's eyes were wide as she continued to circle the urn. "There is no power on Earth that could keep us away."

Acton agreed. "We'll be there, you can count on it." He pushed to his feet. "Now, how does this prove who these people are?"

Antoniou smiled. "Let me paint you a picture." He stepped over to the first excavated body. "I think you are absolutely right about these people. They were noblemen, massacred, and buried with honor, though shackled so their shame would be known throughout eternity." He stepped to the left of the first body and removed a tarp, revealing the skeleton of what appeared to be a child. "And this young boy, unshackled, shows signs of a violent, horrible death." He indicated evidence of crushed bones. "Something happened to this boy, but I think after the events that led to these men being interned here."

Laura joined him. "What makes you say that?"

"The body was laid with care beside the first in this line, and the urn was placed between the two bodies. I think this suggests that these two people, or at a minimum the boy, was of importance to whoever put it here."

"A plausible explanation," agreed Acton, examining the bones, wincing at how painful the death must have been. "Perhaps his son, or a relation of importance."

"Perhaps, or perhaps a relation to this first man. Whoever the boy was, I think the placement of the urn indicates he was important to whoever placed the urn here." Antoniou quickly strode down the long line of dozens of bodies, then stopped beside a tangled mass of bones.

Acton's eyes shot wide at the sight. "What the hell happened here?"

"That is the question, isn't it?" Antoniou pointed at the shackles, binding the skeletons to each other at the wrists. "These men were shackled together, whereas these others only had their own wrists clasped. What does that suggest to you?"

Laura stepped closer. "These men were alive when they were placed here."

Antoniou smiled, clapping his hands together, the sound echoing through the sunken dig site. "Exactly what we thought! These poor souls were still alive, shackled together like prisoners, and simply tossed into a pile to die with their already dead companions." He pointed at several chipped and broken bones. "You can see that they had suffered wounds like the others. This again fits with Plutarch's account."

Acton shook his head. "What a way to go. Depending on the wound, some of them could have survived for days, maybe even weeks, and as each of them died, there'd be even less chance of escape, as the dead weight would keep increasing."

Laura shivered beside him. "How could anyone be so cruel?"

Antoniou nodded solemnly. "I don't know, but remember, these were different times."

Acton agreed. "But we know from history that Megacles and his entire family were banished from Athens for centuries after these events, so obviously the Athenians agreed that this wasn't acceptable."

Antoniou sighed. "Which might be why these bodies were left here, undisturbed, so that those who died so cruelly, could find some peace in death."

Acton surveyed the scene, shaking his head, then turned to Antoniou. "Okay, you've painted your picture. Now, please, show us this proof you've been teasing us with."

Antoniou smiled. He pointed at one body, the skeletal remains appearing to be lying over the others. "Do you notice anything about this one?"

Acton and Laura stepped closer, even Tommy and Mai braving a few extra steps. Acton shook his head. "No."

Laura pointed. "He's not shackled!"

Antoniou clapped. "Exactly! He's the *only* one without shackles besides the boy. And, as you can see, he was placed on top of the other bodies. It is my belief that this man came here after the fact, placed the urn here, then was killed, his body tossed on top of the others who were dead or dying, as one final humiliation."

Acton smiled. "So, you think this man is their leader?"

Antoniou nodded. "I'm convinced of it."

"And you think this man is Cylon himself?"

Antoniou hopped up and down on his toes. "I do!"

Acton grinned. "You said you had proof."

Antoniou led them back to the urn. "What you may not have noticed is that there is an inscription written on the urn. It is very faint, almost gone, but it is there."

Acton leaned forward, unable to see it at first, then as he held a light closer to the urn, he smiled. "I see it, but you're right, it's very faint. It's almost as if it were scratched onto the surface with stone, rather than baked in during the design process."

Antoniou retrieved several pieces of paper sitting nearby. "That's our theory as well." He handed the pages to Acton. "We took some high-resolution photographs, then put them into the computer. After a little manipulation, we were able to reveal what was written."

Acton excitedly grabbed the pages, Laura leaning in close as they both translated the Ancient Greek, Acton's eyes growing wider with each word until he reached the final, enhanced word, a word that could only be a signature.

"Cylon!" Acton spun toward the unshackled corpse, goosebumps rushing over his entire body. "It has to be him!"

Laura grabbed his arm, shaking him with excitement, as Tommy took a step backward, his head on a swivel, his eyes wide. Acton looked at him.

"What's wrong?"

Tommy shivered. "Just looking for red eyes in the dark."

City of Athens

632 BC

Cylon wept. Unabashedly. All reports were that most of his friends were dead, and those that weren't had been badly wounded.

And all had been entombed, dead or alive.

He thanked the gods for that small mercy.

By being entombed, they had at least been afforded some small honor, recognizing their position in society. He wondered if this was to placate him lest he seek revenge. Dishonoring the dead might have exacted a greater retribution, though at this moment, he wanted all the archons dead for their betrayal.

Though he'd settle for just one.

Megacles.

From what he had been told by his supporters within the gathered crowds, Megacles himself had cut the thread then ordered the slaughter, later claiming the thread had broken on its own accord, a sign from Athena that she no longer supported Cylon and his cause.

It was a blasphemy that Megacles must pay for, though at the moment, in his hour of grief, he wasn't certain how to accomplish that. Perhaps he would be forced to leave it to the gods in the afterlife.

Should he seize power one day, he could enact his revenge, but that could be years from now, for he had no base of support from which to rise to power.

"Cylon?"

His heart leaped and he rose to his feet, wiping the tears from his soiled cheeks at his beloved wife's voice. "Over here."

Calliope emerged from the shadows, their clandestine meeting arranged through a friend. He didn't dare return to their home, and he had given her strict instructions to be followed, to ensure she wasn't tracked. She recognized him and rushed forward, collapsing into his arms. "Oh, my love, I feared I would never see you again."

He hugged her hard, burying his nose in her hair, breathing its intoxicating scent in for what might be the last time. "Did you follow my instructions?"

She nodded, staring up at him. "To the letter. I wasn't followed."

"Good." He smiled at her, pinching her chin. "I knew I could rely on you." He held her out in front of him, staring at her with concern. "Have they harmed you?"

She shook her head. "Not in any way. I think they fear what my father might do."

He chuckled. "If they know what's good for them…" He sighed. "Speaking of your father, I think you should leave immediately to stay with him. Right now, they aren't touching you, but I fear what might happen in time."

"And you will come with me."

He frowned. "Eventually. But I have something I must do before I join you."

"And what is that?"

"I need to know if the rumors are true."

"What rumors?"

"That they have entombed some of my people alive with the dead."

She lowered her head, nodding slowly as she stared at the ground. "I've heard the same horrible things." She looked up at him. "Surely they wouldn't do such a thing!"

"Megacles betrayed them when he cut the thread. He is filled with rage, and the others are afraid to challenge him. I fear I may have created a tyrant through my actions." He closed his eyes, picturing his friends and the horror of their last moments. "I need to know if my people still suffer."

"And if they do? The tomb is guarded. There's no way you can free them."

"I don't intend to free them."

She frowned, squeezing his hands tighter. "I don't understand. What do you intend to do?"

"I intend to give them an honorable death."

Dimotiki Agora

Athens, Greece

Present Day

"It's too late."

Damos frowned, his chair protesting loudly as he leaned back, his chest growing tight. He pressed the phone tighter against his ear. "What do you mean?"

"The outsiders I spoke of. They're here, and they brought a security team with them."

Damos' eyes widened.

A security team? Why would archaeologists from America bring a security team?

Something didn't make sense, but explanations were irrelevant. They were here, and it was a problem.

"How many?"

"Six."

He closed his eyes, sighing. "Are they any good?"

"I think so. I think they're former Special Forces or something."

A vein pulsed on his neck. "American?"

"No, Greek."

He drew a deep breath, then opened his eyes. "That complicates things. Can you still get the item?"

"No, not anymore. They're setting up cameras around the perimeter, and searching everyone as they leave. I can still probably get it to where your people were going to retrieve it, but I could get caught."

"That's not my problem, that's yours."

"I'm aware of that, but I think this is too risky now. We're going to have to call it off."

He leaned forward, gripping the phone tightly. "That's not an option."

"What do you mean?"

"Promises have been made. Monies have been paid. If you don't provide what you promised, then those people we spoke of just might decide to eliminate you as punishment."

"Then-then what am I going to do?"

He could hear the fear in her voice, and did have a hint of sympathy for her. She was an amateur, only a thief through circumstance, as opposed to one who actively stole goods from stores or people's houses. If she had never been presented the opportunity, he doubted she'd have ever stolen anything in her life.

But none of that mattered.

For his life was on the line as well.

"Figure it out yourself. These people are either getting what they paid for, or taking you as payment instead."

"I-I'll figure out something."

"You do that."

He ended the call then leaned back, calming his nerves as he debated on whether he should call the team the winning bidder had dispatched for the collection of the item.

He shook his head.

They're liable to kill you first.

The Necropolis

City of Athens

632 BC

Cylon had the distinct impression he had been followed the entire way to the tomb where his friends and supporters had been interned, yet every time he doubled back to catch whomever it was, he came up empty.

Nerves.

It had to be. He was imagining things. He was so on edge that his mind was playing tricks on him, though every fiber of his being was screaming the same thing.

Stop!

It was foolishness what he was doing. He was heading into the belly of the lion. He was certain Megacles had left some of his friends alive to lay a trap for him. The archon had to know it would be an irresistible force that would draw him in. And knowing that fact, made Cylon even more the fool.

Or was it something else?

He wanted to survive for his wife and son's sake, but for what? He had lost everything, and his name would be a stain on his family should he remain at large. His wife was from a good family, a powerful family, and she would go to her father tomorrow, with their son, and they would thrive there, he was certain.

Though only if he were no longer a source of trouble for Athens.

He had to die to save them.

Though first, he must save the souls of his friends.

Again, he heard something behind him and whipped around, finding nothing but empty streets, only the odd candle flickering in but a few windows, this the dead of night.

He drew a steadying breath, now convinced *if* he were being followed, it wasn't a man but a beast, perhaps a stray dog, for the footfalls he was certain he was hearing were too light to be anyone or anything that might challenge him.

He decided to ignore anything further he might hear, and pressed onward toward the tomb. The entrance was well lit, revealing two tired guards and little else.

It surprised him. If they had indeed thought he might return, surely there would be more than two guards.

Now he was on edge.

This had to be a trap. There was no way they would leave so few guards, not with him still at large.

Though if he were wise, as he was certain they thought he was, he would have left the city yesterday, and not returned until he had sufficient forces to stage his coup and take his place as tyrant.

He grunted.

They must not know me, for I am *a fool.*

He crept forward in the dark, nearing the entrance, his head on a swivel as he took in everything around him, trying to make sense of the shadows surrounding him, and the sounds that filled his ears.

And he still found nothing.

Well, you wanted to die.

He stood straight, drawing his sword, then strode with purpose toward the entrance, the two guards, chatting among themselves, not noticing him until he was mere paces away.

"Halt! Identify yourself!"

"I am Cylon of Athens."

Both men stared at him then each other in shock.

It would be their final mistake.

Cylon's blade swung quietly through the air, the torchlight glimmering off the honed metal as it sliced open the belly of the nearest guard, then cleaved the chin of the second on the upswing. He plunged the tip of the weapon into the chest of the second, silencing his scream before it could be uttered, then dropped his heel hard on the neck of the first, ending his groans of agony with the crushing of his windpipe.

It was over in mere seconds, leaving Cylon to seek shelter in the shadows of the entrance as he peered into the darkness for any others lying in wait.

And again, he found none.

He dragged the bodies inside then grabbed one of the torches, hurrying down a long set of steps that then opened into a necropolis of significant size.

And he gasped as his eyes adjusted, and his ears picked up the faint moans of agony that confirmed the horrible rumors.

Megacles' shame knows no bounds!

He rushed forward and stumbled over the first body, a long row of the dead stretching out into the darkness, each shackled to the next, their bodies neatly aligned.

At least some respect was shown.

But these were the dead.

What of the others?

He hurried down the line, holding his torch close to each face, saying their names as he recognized them, followed by a short prayer for each of their souls.

Then he found the source of the anguish he had been hearing. A jumble of bodies, some dead, some writhing in weakened agony, all shackled together in a sickening, twisted mound of flesh as those who still lived tried to escape their tortuous fate.

"Cylon!"

It was barely a whisper, but he'd recognize the voice anywhere.

"Basileios!"

He rushed forward, holding his torch out, searching for his friend, when a hand reached out and grabbed his ankle. He dropped to the ground, taking the hand and following the outstretched arm into the pile of limbs, then pulled, his friend slipping out, covered in the blood of those that had surrounded him, and much of his own from the gaping wound on his back.

"My friend! I can't believe they did this to you."

Basileios stared up at him, his eyes vacant, his face pale. "Kill me."

Cylon shook his head. "No, I'm going to get you out of here. I'm going to get you all out of here."

It hadn't been his plan, though he had never dreamed that not only had Megacles actually committed this horrible crime, but that his best friend would be one of those left alive.

It changed everything.

Basileios shook his head. "I'm dead already. Please, just end our suffering."

A chorus of voices joined him, each echoing the same sentiment, and his chest ached and eyes burned at the impossible deed he was being asked to perform.

"Please, Cylon, kill us!"

"Have mercy!"

"Please, end our suffering!"

His voice cracked as his shoulders shook. "I-I shall, my friends. I shall." Sobs racked his body as he collapsed, praying to the gods for forgiveness for what he was about to do.

He rose, his blade in one hand, the torch in the other, holding the flame to each of the faces in the tangled bunch. The first was dead already, but the second wasn't.

"Kill me!"

"Perseus!" Cylon closed his eyes as he pictured the first time he had met this once powerful man, tears flowing down his cheeks as he prepared himself for what was asked of him.

No man should ever be forced to do such a thing.

He opened his eyes and forced a smile, placing the tip of his blade against Perseus' chest. "Don't worry, my friend, your suffering is almost over."

A hand reached out and touched his arm. "Thank you, my friend."

Cylon shoved the blade hard into Perseus' chest, the last gasp of life from his friend causing Cylon to cry out in anguish, collapsing before the others as his shoulders heaved.

To his shame, the rest were easier, and soon the tangled mess he had found was silent, save his friend, Basileios, whom he had left for last.

"Please. Release me from this hell."

Cylon sat beside his friend, brushing the hair from his eyes. "I'm so sorry I left you."

"It-it was my choice."

"It doesn't make it any easier. It's because of me that you're here."

Basileios' eyes opened with a brief moment of clarity, staring up at him. "Never for a moment think I blame you for what happened. I love you like a brother, and die happy in knowing that it was you, my best friend, that ended my life, rather than a dishonorable wretch like Megacles." He reached forward, weakly gripping Cylon's wrist, dragging the sword toward him. "Now finish this, and save yourself. They will be back."

Cylon nodded, rising to his knees, positioning the blade over his friend's heart. "I will see you soon in Elysium."

Basileios smiled. "I look forward to it."

Cylon closed his eyes and plunged the blade deep through his friend, crying out at his friend's last gasp, then draping himself over the body of the one person who knew everything about him, who knew all his secrets, and who had always been there to support him.

What will I do without you?

He rose, withdrawing his sword, then bent over to pick up the torch. Something glimmered in the light, gripped in his friend's hand. He knelt and pried open the tightly clasped fingers, then gasped.

It was the amulet given him by Pythia.

An amulet that had not provided him with the strength of Apollo, but instead misery and failure at every turn.

He pulled it from his friend's hand then rose, listening for the sounds of any more suffering, instead only hearing the hammering of his own heart.

He took one final look at his fallen friends, bowing his head in prayer, then hurried toward the exit. He had survived, and though he still wanted to die, he had one remaining task before that blessed release.

He had to kill Megacles.

King George Hotel

Athens, Greece

Present Day

It probably redefined quickie, but as Adelaide rolled off him, Leather sensed she was as satisfied as he was, though he didn't dare ask.

"That was a bloody ripper!"

"Is that good?"

She grinned. "Oh yeah."

Leather smiled with relief. "Who knew so much could be packed into five minutes."

She laughed, wrapping a leg over his body and nestling into his shoulder. "This was a tremendous idea. I've always wanted to see Athens." She propped herself up on his chest, staring into his eyes. "Do you think your friends will give me a tour?"

He grunted. "They're not my friends, they're my clients."

"But I thought you said they were nice?"

"They are. Very. But they're still my clients. I like them, yes, but I can't risk the lines being blurred."

She ran a finger down his chest, toward his nether regions. "I think this little idea of your client suggests the line is already blurred."

He frowned. "You're right." He sighed, closing his eyes as her finger reached more sensitive topics. "Umm, as much as I hate to say this, I have to get ready."

Squeeze.

"Are you sure?"

He moaned. "You have no idea how much I want to cancel my contract right now."

She laughed, giving one last squeeze, then releasing—much to his disappointment and relief. "Go, get ready. I'll keep myself entertained."

"You're the best."

"I know, and don't you forget it."

He rolled out of bed and made for the bathroom, a smile on his face. "I wouldn't dare."

"Your phone is vibrating."

He hurried back to find the phone nestled between her breasts. "Phone call for Mr. Leather, paging Mr. Leather."

He grinned, then straddled her stomach and retrieved the phone. "It's Korba." He swiped his thumb. "Hello?"

"Five minutes."

Something started down below. "Umm, can you find some traffic?"

"Huh?"

"I need fifteen."

"I'll wait. She better be gorgeous."

The call ended and he groaned. "You're terrible." He looked down at her. "And I mean that in the most wonderful way."

She winked, and gave him an unforgettable send-off before he finally threw himself together and met Korba in front of the hotel. He climbed in with a smile.

"Your definition of fifteen minutes is different than mine, my friend."

Leather chuckled, shaking the man's hand, noticing the grip slightly different than expected before he remembered Korba's missing pinky finger. "Sorry about that. What's the status?"

"The site is secure. We're putting up surveillance equipment now. Cameras, motion detectors, lighting, a more robust screening process. Everything should be online within a couple of hours."

"Excellent. Resistance?"

Korba shrugged. "Some of the younger people are a little upset at the pat downs, especially the women. I have a couple of females coming in tomorrow with the rest of my team. I figured it was more important to get an advance team on-site first."

Leather nodded. "You made the right choice. If the women object, just have them search each other." He paused. "Doesn't the professor in charge have his wife on-site? Maybe she could do the pat downs, just in case there are more than one involved in the thefts. We wouldn't want the thieves patting down each other."

Korba made a left, cursing at the light he just ran. "That's a good idea." He took an exaggerated sniff of the air between them. "That's a lovely perfume you're wearing."

"Hey, don't ask, don't tell."

Korba laughed. "Buddy, this is Greece. You better man up, even if you're living an alternative lifestyle."

Leather wagged a finger. "Not that there's anything wrong with that, but how long have you known me?"

"So, it's a woman that had me waiting for so long."

"Yes."

"Name?"

"Adelaide."

"Hair?"

"Blond."

"Tits?"

"Two, and if you ask me anything else like that, I'll tear off your other finger to match."

Korba tossed his head back, laughing. "You definitely haven't changed. Chivalrous as always, even toward that horrible ex-wife of yours."

Leather rolled his eyes. "Let's not bring her into this. There was a time I'd prefer castration to the very idea of another long-term relationship."

"So, you think this one could be the one?"

Leather shrugged. "Waaay too early to tell. Let's just say she's fantastic, and a lot of fun. But we've spent a grand total of three days together, four if you count today."

"A lifetime!"

Leather eyed him. "For you, perhaps. How many marriages was it?"

Korba started counting off on his fingers. "I stopped after four." He held up his digit deprived hand. "But only because I can't count any higher."

Dimotiki Agora

Athens, Greece

Damos' heart skipped a beat when the call was answered. He shouldn't have taken the job of finding a buyer for an item like this. It was too expensive. When the money was in the eight figures, it meant men like those he was now on the line with.

It meant death was around a corner too close.

"You have to go in tonight."

"Why?"

"By tomorrow there will be too many guards."

"How many are there now?"

He took a chance, one he had a feeling he might regret later. "Just those that were already there. Amateurs. You'll have no problem handling them. She says the item will be where she previously indicated."

"She?"

106

"Yes."

"Your contact is a woman?"

His chest tightened with the disgust on the other end of the line. "Yes. Is that a problem?"

"You expect us to trust a woman?"

Damos closed his eyes, shaking his head, repulsed by the tone. "This isn't the Islamic State. Here we trust our women."

The rage in response had him nearly evacuating his bowels. "I should slit your throat for your blasphemy!"

His chin trembled as sweat trickled down his back, wondering what had possessed him to be so stupid. "I apologize. I meant no disrespect. What I meant is that here we trust our women, right or wrong, and I trust that she is telling me the truth. You have to go in tonight, or you'll never get in."

There was a pause, the only sounds the bursts of static from heavy breathing near the mouthpiece. "Very well. But if she's lying, *you're* the one who will pay the price."

The call ended and Damos collapsed in his chair, almost blacking out from the panic attack now threatening to overwhelm him. He had dealt with criminals most of his life, and few scared him. But these weren't criminals. These were fanatics, out to make a profit to fund their insane dream of a worldwide caliphate.

And they wouldn't hesitate to kill him, should things go wrong.

God, please let nothing go wrong.

Phaleron Delta Necropolis
Athens, Greece

Acton smiled broadly as their head of security, Cameron Leather, entered the dig site, accompanied by his Greek counterpart. Laura rushed up to him, arms extended, giving him a quick double-cheek kiss, the poor man appearing as uncomfortable as their friend Hugh Reading did every time someone tried the move on him.

Though he never minded it with Laura.

You never mind getting hugged and kissed by your daughter.

And he was certain that was how their friend thought of Laura after all these years, though if you ever suggested he was old enough to be her father, he'd give you a withering stink-eye until you recanted.

"Is your friend settled in at the hotel?"

Korba grunted. "I'll say, I think they broke the bed already."

Without looking, Leather's hand snapped out, stopping a hair's breadth from the Greek's happy place.

"I'll go check on my men." Korba retreated quickly, and Leather returned his attention to Laura and the others, all stifling grins.

"Yes, she is. Thank you so much for allowing me to bring her."

Acton stepped forward, trying his best to ignore the awkward smile on the man's face.

He's got it bad.

"You should bring her by for a tour, if that's okay with you, Professor."

Antoniou nodded vigorously. "Of course! Of course! Bring her! We would be happy to give her the VIP treatment."

Leather smiled. "That would be wonderful. I know she'd be chuffed to see something like this. In fact, she had already jokingly asked me to find out if it were okay."

Laura patted his arm. "Of course it is. Any friend of yours is a friend of ours."

Leather turned all business. "Darius tells me that his men should be set up before midnight, so within the next couple of hours. Once the equipment comes online, we should have complete perimeter security. With the handheld scanners and pat downs, we should put an end to your little problem here."

Antoniou sighed. "I hope so. It's so distressing!" He gestured toward the table holding the urn with Cylon's warning etched on it. "I'm just thankful that this wasn't stolen."

Leather's eyes narrowed and he strode over to the table, making a quick circuit of the area. "It's valuable?"

The doubt in his voice had Acton chuckling. "After all these years of working with us, don't you know by now that it isn't just precious metals and gems that have value?"

Leather shrugged. "Looks like something my grandmother might have in her sitting room."

Tommy snorted. "I think I saw one just like it at Pier 1."

Mai blushed, giving Tommy an elbow to the ribs, silencing him. "How long have you been waiting to say that?"

"Two hours," replied a wincing Tommy.

Acton gave him a covert thumbs up, mouthing, "Good one!" before giving Leather a quick explanation. "Have you heard of Cylon?"

Leather nodded. "Yeah, isn't that the homeworld of a race of cybernetic organisms that rebelled against the human race?"

Tommy snickered.

"Yes it is, and do you know where they got their name?"

Leather paused. "Umm, I had always assumed it was short for cybernetic something."

"And you'd be wrong. Actually, if you watch the original Battlestar Galactica, you'll notice that it was heavily influenced by Ancient Greece. Apollo, Athena, Greek-styled helmets for the Viper pilots, and an enemy called Cylons. Most people don't realize that Cylon was a real person from the seventh century BC Athens. He tried to stage a coup, and failed." Acton motioned at the scores of skeletons nearby. And we believe these are his followers, and this"—he pointed at the skeleton he was now convinced was the man himself—"is Cylon, their leader."

Leather whistled, his head slowly bobbing. "So, I assume that makes this find of significant importance?"

"It confirms one of the first recorded events in Ancient Greek history." Acton gestured toward the urn. "And *this*, is the proof. This urn appears to have been inscribed by Cylon himself, and we believe was placed in here by him after his followers were entombed here, some still alive. And we believe he then died here, in battle, before he could escape."

Leather shook his head. "I'd hate to disagree with you, but if you'll forgive an amateur's perspective, I'd like to offer a theory of my own."

Acton, slightly surprised, smiled. "Please do."

"I won't dispute anything you said except your last statement." He stepped over to the skeleton that they believed was Cylon, and knelt, as if in reverence. "If I had led these people to their deaths, and had heard that some had been left alive in here to die, I would have done anything I could to get to them. And if saving them wasn't an option, I would have ended their suffering, then stood my ground, fighting any and all who would dishonor their memory, until I was finally struck down." He reached out and touched Cylon's hand, his voice barely a whisper. "Only then could I live with the shame of what I had done."

Acton's chest tightened at the emotion in Leather's voice, and it made him wonder if something had happened in the man's past of which they weren't aware. Laura stepped over to him, placing a hand on the man's shoulder. "A beautiful sentiment." Leather rose, and she gave him a quick hug before turning to the others. "I think we have a new theory to add to the mix. Did Cylon fail in an escape attempt, or did he stand his ground and fight to the death, dying willingly?" She flashed a smile at Leather. "I'm inclined to believe the latter."

Acton nodded, scratching his chin. "Sometimes you need a soldier's perspective to understand the motivations of another soldier." He grunted. "I like it. Too bad we couldn't go back in time and be a fly on the wall here."

Tommy raised a finger. "Well, speaking of time travel—"

Acton held up a hand, cutting him off as he spun toward the ramp. "Did you hear that?"

More popping sounds, then a scream. A burst of static erupted from Leather's comm gear.

"We're under attack!"

Acton spun toward Tommy and Mai, pointing toward a large tarp covering a yet to be excavated area. "Get under there and stay quiet until we come for you."

Tommy stood frozen for a moment, then grabbed Mai, pulling the terrified woman toward the feeble cover as Acton followed Leather and the others toward the entrance, the gunfire growing more intense. Laura disappeared over the top then screamed, a body rolling down the temporary ramp.

Acton sprinted toward it, the uniform identifying the victim as one of Korba's men. He paused to check him. "Are you okay?"

He nodded. "Took them in the vest." He thrust a weapon into Acton's hands. "Go!"

Acton didn't need to be told twice. He rushed up the ramp, readying the weapon, and spotted Laura lying nearby, behind one of Korba's

SUVs. His heart almost stopped and he was about to cry out when he spotted muzzle fire erupting from under the vehicle, coming from a weapon under her control.

She was okay.

He pressed up against the wall near the top of the ramp, surveying the scene. Several of Korba's men were down, and the remainder of the gunfire was being directed toward the main gate, at least a dozen muzzles flashing at them, revealing their superior numbers.

And their positions.

He checked on the others, deciding they were all behind solid cover, then slinked along the side of the embankment that housed the dig site, and away from the gunfight. Out of sight, he sprinted along the side then around the back, finally climbing to the top of one of the berms and taking up a position that gave him a clear view of the front gate. He lay prone, crawling into his final position, then made sure his weapon was on single shot.

He had no extra magazines.

He took aim and fired, the man dropping. He fired again, this time missing, his chest heaving too hard to aim properly. He steadied himself then fired once more, and another dropped from a hit to the leg.

And finally they took notice of the new angle of attack.

Several turned to fire, and he switched to full-auto, emptying the rest of the mag into the cluster of attackers in short, controlled bursts, then rolled away, the safety of the berm protecting him from the returned fire. Safe, he rushed back the way he had come, kicking himself for not taking more than the weapon when it had been offered him.

As he rounded the final corner, about to enter the parking area, engines roared and the gunfire dwindled then stopped.

"All clear!" shouted Leather, and Acton breathed a sigh of relief before raising his hands.

"Friendly on your six!" he shouted, emerging tentatively from around the corner, his gun over his head. Weapons spun toward him then quickly lowered, and he picked up his pace when he was certain he wouldn't be blown away. "Is everyone okay?"

Laura stood, dusting herself off. "I'm fine. Basil? Juno?"

Antoniou emerged from behind a stack of boxes, clearly shaken. "I-I'm okay. Juno? Where are you?"

Juno emerged from behind a row of vehicles, her cheek scratched and knee bleeding. "I-I'm fine. Just a little banged up."

Antoniou rushed over to her, as did Laura, while Acton joined Leather and Korba, tending to the downed members of the Greek team.

"Are they okay?"

Korba shook his head, making the sign of the cross as he held a hand to the chest of one of his men. Leather replied for him. "He didn't make it. Took one to the neck."

Acton dropped to a knee, closing his eyes as the moans of pain surrounding him threatened to overwhelm him. Then his eyes shot wide. "Mai!" He leaped to his feet and sprinted toward the site entrance. He rushed down the ramp and toward the tarp. "Are you guys okay?"

The tarp moved then two heads appeared. "Yup," replied Tommy. "Is everyone okay?"

Acton shook his head. "At least one of the guards is dead, and several are wounded pretty bad. But you two are okay, right?"

They both nodded, tears streaming down Mai's face. "Professor Palmer?"

Acton gave her a hard hug eagerly returned. "She's okay. You know her. I think she singlehandedly fought them off."

Mai giggled, still holding on, and he felt no compulsion to release his own grip. He reached out and squeezed Tommy's shoulders. "Thanks for watching out for her."

He shrugged. "It's kinda my job now, isn't it?"

Mai reached out and pulled him into the hug, and the three of them stood there for a moment, saying nothing, when Acton's eyes shot wide and his jaw dropped at the sight before him.

"Oh my God! It's gone!" He let go of his young charges and rushed toward the table that had held the urn inscribed by Cylon, then examined the ground for broken shards, finding none. He spun toward Tommy and Mai. "Did you see who took it?"

They both shook their heads, Tommy replying. "Sorry, sir, but we didn't see anything. Our heads were covered."

"Did you hear anything?"

Again, they both shook their heads. "Only gunfire. I was just trying to stay quiet and not piss myself."

Acton again surveyed the area for any evidence of the precious relic, then sprinted up the ramp and into the parking lot where the others were. He jogged over to where Laura was, Antoniou and Juno with her, watching as police and paramedics arrived.

"It's gone."

They all turned toward him. "What's gone?" asked Laura, then she gasped. "You don't mean…"

He nodded. "The urn is gone."

Antoniou's eyes widened and he wobbled. Acton reached out and grabbed him by the arms to steady him. "It-it can't be. We stopped them. We stopped them at the gate."

Acton shook his head. "I checked the area. It didn't fall off and break. Someone physically took it." He threw a hand toward the scene before them. "All this must have been a diversion. While we were watching the gate, someone else must have come into the dig site and taken it." He sighed, his eyes closing as he pictured the dead and wounded. "All of this for nothing."

Leather walked over, his face grim, his hands and clothes covered in blood, an active participant in the first aid being provided. "You're all fine?"

Laura nodded. "And Darius' men?"

"One dead, four wounded. They'll live, but they're out of the game. We'll be short staffed until replacements arrive tomorrow."

Acton frowned. "It doesn't much matter now."

Leather's eyes narrowed. "What do you mean?"

"The urn was stolen during the attack."

116

Leather stepped to the edge of the dig site, peering into the excavated area. Tommy waved. "Did they see anything?"

"No, I had them hide under a tarp. They didn't hear anything either."

Leather cursed, turning to look at the carnage now tended to by the emergency personnel. "It was all a trick." He kicked at the stone covered parking lot, sending a small rock skittering across the ground toward one of the parked cars. "Clever, though costly."

Acton stared at the gate. "How many of theirs did we get?"

"Six."

His eyebrows shot up. "Six? Maybe one of them knows where it was taken."

Leather shook his head. "They're all dead."

Acton's eyes narrowed. "But I know I shot one in the leg. I guess they took him with them when they left."

Leather shook his head. "No, they killed their wounded."

Bile filled Acton's mouth. "Unbelievable. Who are these people?"

"I took photos of all their faces before the police arrived. I've sent them to your phone. I suggest forwarding them to Agent Reading, just in case the authorities here aren't so forthcoming."

Acton agreed. "Good idea."

Leather handed him a phone. "And I found this on one of the bodies." He nodded toward Tommy, now approaching with Mai. "I suggest you give it to the whiz kid and see what he finds."

"Give me what?" asked Tommy.

Acton handed him the phone. "We might have been talking about another whiz kid."

Tommy grinned. "How many do you actually know?" He stared toward the main gate. "Is this one of theirs?"

"Yes. Tuck it away somewhere, then when we get back to the hotel, work your magic."

Tommy stuffed it into an inner pocket of his jacket. "Consider it done."

Antoniou stared at the pocket. "Do-do you think you can find something that can help us? We have to recover the urn, we have to find out who is behind this." He threw up his hands, color returning to his cheeks. "This is a disaster! The history that has been lost!" He reached out for Juno, tears staining her cheeks. "They'll shut us down for sure!"

Acton stepped closer to his friend. "It wasn't your fault."

A burst of air erupted from Antoniou's mouth. "That may be true, but in today's Greece, someone always has to be blamed, so long as the government isn't. If we had proper funding, we'd have had proper security in place, and the petty thefts would never have happened, and whoever is behind this wouldn't have been so emboldened to steal the prize."

Leather cleared his throat. "Are we sure it's the same people?"

Laura's eyes narrowed. "Who else could it be?"

"Well, before, you said it was always just little things, with no one getting hurt. No violence whatsoever, right?"

Antoniou nodded. "That's correct. Always something that could be tucked away easily somewhere. And no one ever got hurt."

"Right. Now we have this direct assault, in numbers, heavily armed. That doesn't match the previous thefts at all. And frankly, I don't understand the value of these things very well, but I can't see what had been stolen being profitable enough to warrant a team that expensive."

Acton grunted. "You're absolutely right, up until a few days ago, when they discovered that urn. On the black market, it could be worth quite a lot."

Antoniou agreed. "I'd estimate millions to the right person."

Tommy's eyes bulged. "Millions? That old pot we were looking at?"

Antoniou turned toward him. "Yes. Remember, it's not what it's made of that gives it its value. It's the history. A well-preserved ancient urn isn't necessarily worth that much, but one with an inscription from Cylon himself, with contents that are a mystery?" He threw his hands up. "Who knows what it could be worth to the right person?"

Acton pursed his lips. "Who knew about it?"

Antoniou shook his head. "Everyone did. You can't hide excitement like that. We told everyone to keep it quiet, but you know young people, they probably had it all over their phones before they left the site."

Leather gestured toward the gate. "There's something more going on here, though. All these guys looked Middle Eastern. Could the Muslims somehow have taken offense to what you're doing here?"

Acton's eyebrows rose. "You mean that this wasn't a theft, but an attack?"

Leather shrugged. "You don't assault a site the way they did, unless you intend to inflict damage. This was not a surgical operation, it was a sloppy mess."

Acton frowned. "Yet they still succeeded."

Leather exhaled loudly. "You're right. If the urn was still here, then my theory that this was a terrorist attack might hold water, but since it's gone, it does suggest that this was a heist after all."

"It was a reasonable theory, especially based upon past experience."

Antoniou nodded. "It's always a constant fear with archaeological finds today that should they somehow contradict the Koran, someone will take offense and try to kill you for your troubles. They're so easily provoked." He shook his head, holding up a hand. "I'm sorry, that was uncalled for."

"Even if it's the truth," muttered Tommy.

Acton regarded him for a moment, the young man's observations unfortunately closer to the truth than the political class would have them believe.

"Sorry," mumbled Tommy. "I guess *that* was uncalled for too." He patted his pocket where the phone was hidden. "Hopefully this will give us some answers."

Acton nodded. "Hopefully."

They all turned as Korba approached. "I'm glad to see you're all okay. My men are on their way to the hospital. Fortunately, your own guards ran at the first sign of trouble, so they're fine, but I doubt you'll get them to come back."

120

Antoniou frowned. "Then we've got no one to protect the site tonight."

Korba shook his head, gesturing at the heavy police presence. "Don't worry. Nobody is getting in or out of this place without going through them. They'll be here for a while."

Antoniou breathed a sigh of relief. "That's good." He groaned. "There'll be no hiding what's been going on here now." His shoulders slumped. "It's over."

Korba jerked a thumb over his shoulder. "You'll have to excuse me. They're trying to blame my guys for what happened, saying we were overreacting to petty thieves." He spat. "Petty thieves don't carry AKs."

Acton watched as a body bag was zipped up with Korba's man inside. "We can't seem to go anywhere without someone dying."

"It's the curse."

They all turned to Juno, her face pale.

"What do you mean?" asked Laura.

"It's the curse that Cylon wrote on the urn. It's coming true once again."

Acton shuddered as he recalled the words inscribed by the would-be tyrant, then wrapped an arm around Laura's shoulders. "Let's hope the paranormal doesn't begin to enter this. If it does, then we're truly screwed."

King George Hotel
Athens, Greece

Acton leafed through the New York Times International Edition as he sipped his orange juice, Laura sitting beside him buttering a croissant. A knock at the door had him folding the paper, Laura waving him off.

"I'll get it."

"Check first."

"Yes, Daddy."

"Ooh, who's your daddy?"

She gave him the eye. "I've always thought that was one of the most disgusting phrases ever uttered."

He chuckled. "Agreed. Never understood it myself, unless the girl has serious daddy issues."

Laura peered through the peephole then unlocked the door. "Even then, what kind of guy asks it?"

"Someone with issues."

"Who asks what?" asked Tommy as he and Mai entered.

"Who's your daddy?"

Tommy laughed. "The first time I asked her, she thought I wanted to know his name!"

Mai blushed, belting his arm, Tommy genuinely feeling the pain this time. "No bedroom talk!"

His shoulders sagged, and he truly did appear contrite. "Sorry, hon, that was wrong."

She took her seat, giving him the cold shoulder, and Acton gave Laura a surreptitious wink. He tossed the Times aside and opened the Greek To Vima paper delivered with their breakfast, struggling to translate the headline, when his jaw slackened.

"Uh oh."

Laura looked at him. "What?"

"Well, my Ancient Greek is far better than my modern, but they do say a picture is worth a thousand words." He turned the front page around so they could see the photo that had him concerned.

A photo of the dig site, with an inset of the missing urn.

"What's it say?" asked Mai.

Acton frowned. "Got an hour?"

Tommy motioned for him to hand over the newspaper. "Give it here."

Acton gave him a look.

"Please."

Acton gave an exaggerated nod of his head. "That's better." He handed it over and Tommy pulled out his phone, taking a photo of the front page. A few taps of the screen and he handed the phone to Acton. His eyebrows shot up. "Holy crap!"

Laura leaned over. "What?"

"It's the article. Translated." He pulled his phone out of his pocket and handed it to Tommy. "Whatever app just did that, install it."

Tommy grinned. "It's actually a custom thing I whipped together."

Acton eyed him. "So, what, you want me to pay you?"

Tommy's eyes bulged. "Would you?"

Acton chuckled. "If it's good, then why not turn it into an app and sell it?"

Tommy looked at Mai. "What do you think? Should I?"

She shrugged, there still a hint of an Arctic front between them. "I always said you should."

Acton scanned the article, impressed with the accuracy. "You never know, it could turn into some extra pocket change, or a full-fledged business." He gestured toward his phone. "But just start charging *after* you've installed it on my phone."

Laura slid hers across the table. "And mine. I wouldn't want to have to charge you for your hotel room."

Tommy blushed and Mai's jaw dropped, her ears crimson. Horrified glances were exchanged, the cold air mass gone as they were once again a united front. Tommy's eyes darted everywhere except Laura's direction. "Umm, well, we can pay, but, umm—"

Acton laughed. "*No*, you can't. This is a five-star hotel, and costs more a night than you make in a week." He reached out and gave Laura a playful slap on the shoulder. "Now look what you've done."

Laura reached out and patted Tommy's knee. "I was just joking. You know you're always welcome to travel with us, and it will never cost you a dime." She tapped her phone. "As long as we keep getting free apps."

Tommy smiled. "Deal, though I think we're coming out waaay ahead."

Acton grunted. "Don't worry. When you earn your first billion and are richer than us, you can pay for everything."

Tommy's smile broadened. "Now *that's* a deal."

Acton waved Tommy's phone. "According to this, what happened last night is obviously big news. It looks like one of the grad students that was there spilled everything, including about the shootout, the deaths, and everything about the stolen urn. It also tells about the petty thefts that had been going on, and the fact it had been covered up by Professor Antoniou." He shook his head. "This is terrible. Basil is going to be devastated."

Laura took the phone, skimming the article for herself. "The cover-up is what's going to get them shut down. Even if we help fund the excavation, with the deaths and the lies, I don't know if that would be enough."

Tommy swallowed a piece of bacon. "But isn't it important?"

Laura returned his phone. "As you get older, you'll come to realize that the first things that get cut when budgets are tight, are the arts and sciences. Unfortunately, digging up ancient bones and clay pots pales, and perhaps rightly so, when the choice is discovery versus more nurses or police officers."

Acton refilled his coffee. "This is why private donations are so important. If it's important to the people, then things will get funded themselves, without having to use taxpayers' money. Throughout history, this was how the arts were funded, and how charities were funded. Governments didn't provide subsidies, it was the wealthy that gave money to help the poor. It was their responsibility as nobles. Today, the rich give billions, but too many who control the microphones vilify them for being rich, without looking at what they do for the poor, or for science in general." He flicked a wrist toward his wife. "Look at Laura. She's donated—"

"We've donated."

He chuckled. "Fine. *We've* donated, millions upon millions. And when she kicks the bucket before me, I'm going to party like it's 1999, then leave what's left to charity, and join her wherever she ended up."

She gave him a look. "Party too hard, and we might just end up heading in opposite directions."

Acton pursed his lips, his head bobbing slowly. "This is true. Perhaps I better die first."

"Well, you are much older than me."

His eyebrows rose and his head dipped forward. "Much?"

"Don't worry, dear, you wear it well."

Mai sighed, taking Tommy's hand as she watched the exchange. "I hope we end up like you two. You're so funny."

Acton smiled at her. "If it's meant to be, then you will be. But remember, it takes time to get comfortable with a person, and it's a lot tougher when you're younger and still discovering who you are."

Laura agreed. "Give it time, and you'll know what each other is thinking."

Acton grinned. "And if those thoughts don't terrify you, then maybe you'll be as disgustingly happy as us."

Tommy gave Mai's hand a squeeze. "Sounds good to me." He handed both phones back. "You've been upgraded. Just launch the Triple-T app, take a photo of whatever you want translated, select the language if it can't figure it out by itself, then off you go."

Acton's eyes narrowed. "Triple-T?"

"Tommy's Text Translator."

"Cool." Acton tapped the phone. "See, you've already got a catchy name. Now go turn it into some money. Put those skills to work."

"Oh, that reminds me." Tommy reached into his pocket and pulled out the phone discovered last night on one of the bodies. "I was able to pull some data off the phone. Just the last few calls. It looks like it was a burner calling other burners. Maybe if you get the numbers to Agent Reading, he can run them down."

Acton cursed. "I forgot to send those photos Cameron took." He gestured toward the phone Tommy was holding. "Send me everything you've got, and I'll forward it to Hugh. Maybe he can run them down." He smiled as an idea occurred to him, and he turned to Laura. "Maybe we should invite Hugh to join us."

She swallowed the last of her croissant. "I don't think he has as much vacation time as you think he does. One of these days they're going to fire him."

Acton grunted. "Might be the best thing for him. We'll put him in the spare bedroom."

Laura laughed. "Oh no! It would be like having my father around!"

"I'll tell him you said that."

"Don't you dare! It would gut him!"

Acton smiled at her. "Hon, I don't think you realize this, but I'm pretty sure he already thinks of you as a daughter, not a sister. I think he'd be extremely proud to know you thought of him that way."

She stared at him. "You think?"

"Yup. Then he'd tear you a new one for thinking he was that old."

Reading Residence, Whitehall

London, England

Interpol Agent Hugh Reading woke, immediately grabbing for the small of his back, the recurring aches and pains of old age getting worse by the day. He glanced at the alarm clock and cursed, there still another hour before he wanted to get up. He lay back down, his CPAP mask sucking at his face, and tried to force himself back to sleep.

But his back was having none of that.

A string of expletives that would make a sailor blush erupted, muffled by the mask, as he rolled his legs out of bed. He reached over and turned off the machine, tearing the mask from his face and tossing it onto the nightstand. He hated the fact he had to wear it, but he loved the machine that was saving his life, and had restored his energy levels to near normal.

He was now almost evangelical about it. Whenever a friend or colleague talked about snoring, he'd tell them to get themselves—or their loved one, depending upon who was complaining—checked for sleep apnea. Until he had been diagnosed, he had no idea that it could cause heart damage that could eventually kill you. Why that fact wasn't advertised, he had no idea. Too many people thought snoring was simply an annoyance to the other person in bed with them. Almost none knew it was slowly killing the person by thickening the heart wall.

He reached for his phone as he rubbed the sleep from his eyes, then smiled when he saw a message from his best friend, Jim Acton. He opened the text and frowned when he saw the attached information.

Bloody hell!

He quickly forwarded the information to his partner at Interpol, Michelle Humphrey, then called her, knowing she was planning on being in early today.

"Hugh, what are you doing up so early? I thought you were planning on some beauty sleep. God knows you need it."

He grunted. "Good morning to you too." He tilted his head to the side, cracking his neck. "I just sent you a message with some numbers and photos. Can you run them for me?"

"Just a sec." There was a pause, then the creaking of office furniture and the tapping of keys. "Okay, got it. What's this about?"

"Jim and Laura are in it again."

"These numbers are mostly in Greece."

"Yeah, they're in Athens right now, according to his message."

There was a long sigh. "Please tell me they weren't involved in that gun battle last night."

Reading tensed. "What gun battle?"

"Some armed group attacked an archaeological dig in Athens last night. Some people were killed, some wounded. Some priceless artifact was stolen."

"Bloody hell! If I know them, that's exactly what they're involved with. Run those numbers and photos as fast as you can, and contact Athens to find out the latest. I'm coming in."

"On your day off?"

"There's never a day off when those two are allowed out of the country."

Outside Riyadh, Kingdom of Saudi Arabia

Sheik Khalid bin Al Jabar gripped the arm of his custom designed throne with his free hand. All the joy he felt while sitting within this priceless piece of art built by King Frederick of Prussia and given as a gift to Tsar Peter the Great, had been drained from him.

For he was being lied to.

And he hated being lied to.

"I want my item!"

"But we don't have it. Their security was far stronger than we were led to believe. We lost a lot of good men last night, and it was all for nothing."

"Bullshit!" He grabbed one of several newspapers sitting beside him, shaking it in his hand. "Have you picked up a paper today? It's front page news all across Europe. The urn was stolen last night during the attack. I want what's mine, or there will be consequences!"

"But I swear to Allah that we do not have it."

Khalid saw red, his chest heaving with rage. "You should never have crossed me. Now you will learn what happens when you betray me."

He ended the call then whipped the phone across the room, instantly regretting the impulsive action as it slammed against a panel worth over a million dollars. "Nadeem!"

His manservant immediately appeared. "Sir?"

"Get me Tankov."

Suqut Brigade Safe House
Athens, Greece

Ahmed Rafiq stared at the phone in disbelief, then tossed it on the table in front of him, the OtterBox case protecting it. He frowned at the survivors of last night's fiasco.

"What?" asked Mustafa, his trusted friend and second-in-command.

"He thinks we have it."

"Why would he think that?"

"Apparently, it's in all the papers. It was stolen last night during the attack." He pointed at one of his men, the gofer of the group. "Go get me a copy of today's paper. Something I can read, not that Greek gibberish." The man immediately left.

Mustafa shook his head. "We've been betrayed. That's the only explanation."

"Yes, but by whom? The only people who knew we were coming were the fence Damos, and his contact on the inside."

Mustafa scratched his thick beard. "Unless one of them told someone."

"If they did, then they'd know who they told. Either way, we're dead unless we can deliver it."

"But surely we can reason with the sheik."

Rafiq stared at his friend. "We attacked the place in order to steal the item, and the item was stolen. What would you believe if you were him?"

"We're dead then." Mustafa grunted, jabbing a finger at him. "This is your fault."

Rafiq bristled. "How do you figure?"

"You planned the operation."

"How was I supposed to know they had heavily armed, well-trained guards?"

"It's called reconnaissance. You should have known."

"I checked the night before. You were with me! Those guards weren't there."

"Obviously a lot can change in twenty-four hours, and now six of our team is dead because of you."

Rafiq, seething with rage at the betrayal shown by a man he thought his friend, pulled his Vektor CP1 semiautomatic and put two holes in Mustafa's chest. "Make that seven." He placed his pistol on the table, turning to the shocked team that remained. "Now, what are we going to do about this?"

Everybody nervously eyed each other, none daring speak.

"Forget him. I asked, what are we going to do about this? I need ideas."

Zaman, a competent member of the cause, tentatively raised a finger. "Umm, well, someone stole it."

Rafiq stared at him, unimpressed. "Obviously."

"And it wasn't us."

"I'm beginning to think you're wasting my time."

Zaman paled. "Well, if it was stolen, and we didn't do it, then someone else obviously did."

"You're telling me nothing I don't already know."

"Yes, but who did it? The Russians the sheik usually uses?"

Rafiq grunted. "I doubt that. They lost the job. And from what I understand, they're not the type that would go and complete a contract they lost, just to prove themselves."

Zaman nodded. "Exactly. I think somebody piggybacked off our operation."

Rafiq was about to dismiss whatever came out of Zaman's mouth as idiocy, but stopped, instead letting the train of thought play out. "They would have had to know we were coming, and when."

"Yes. Damos the fence knew. We had to tell him, so he could tell the inside man."

"Woman."

Zaman spit. "It was probably her, the bloody kafir."

"Possibly." Rafiq pursed his lips, leaning back in his chair, his fingers drumming on his thigh. "Damos seemed nervous when I talked to him."

Zaman chuckled. "You tend to make people nervous."

Rafiq grinned, tugging at his beard. "This does seem to make Westerners nervous, doesn't it?"

"They're pathetic and weak."

"True, though perhaps not Damos. He is, after all, a criminal, and in our line of work."

"Perhaps he wanted us to fail so it didn't interfere with his little operation he's had going there."

Rafiq shook his head. "I can't see it. Our success would have kept him in business. Now, he's likely to die."

"Yes, but this was a big score. I think he sent his own people in to grab it, while we were attacking. That way he gets more than a finder's fee."

Rafiq's head slowly bobbed. "Possible, but again, he'd have to know if we found out, he'd die. Horribly. And his finder's fee is already more than he's probably made in the past five years. This is an eight-figure deal. Would he risk his share of that?"

Zaman frowned. "If it's not him, then it has to be the woman on the inside. There's no other possibility."

Rafiq leaned forward. "She knows when we're coming. The attack starts, she takes the artifact as she was supposed to, and places it where she said she was going to. The attack fails, and she takes the opportunity to complete the job herself, cutting us out of the deal."

"Then who does she take it to?"

"Damos."

Zaman grunted. "So, we're back to him again." He scratched behind his ear. "I think we have to pick him up and find out who this woman is. One of the two of them stole from us, it has to be."

There was a coded knock at the door then it opened, the gofer carrying a bunch of papers, dropping them on the table. "It's all over the news. The radio is talking about it non-stop." He sank into his chair, his cheeks flush with excitement. "And I think I know who did it."

Rafiq stared at the gofer. "Please, enlighten us."

"The guy running it."

Rafiq's eyebrows shot up. "Huh?"

"Apparently, there's been funding problems. You know how messed up this country is. His wife has been out fundraising non-stop, and now there's talk of shutting it down until they can figure out what's going on there. I think he's the one who stole it. Think about it. If he takes advantage of the situation, hides it somewhere and sneaks it out later, he can sell it on the black market, and get enough money to fund his dig."

"That'd be pretty ballsy."

The gofer's head bobbed furiously. "Yeah, but those scientist types are nuts. They'll do anything to keep their work going." He shrugged. "At least that's what I've heard."

Zaman snorted. "That's what you've seen in the movies."

Rafiq leaped to his feet, pacing the small room as he pulled at his hair. "I'm through guessing." He spun toward his team. "This is what we're going to do."

Unknown Location

Alexie Tankov stared at the call display, the routing system that made any calls to or from his phone impossible to trace, identifying who was on the other end of the line.

He smiled, then answered the call. "I told you you'd be calling me. What's happened?"

The anger in the sheik's voice was out of character, indicating a man out of control. And dangerous. "The item was retrieved, but they're denying they have it."

Tankov chuckled, already fully aware of what had happened, the news unavoidable. "You expected something more from terrorists?"

"I want them dead, and the item recovered and delivered to me. Double your normal price." There was a pause filled by heavy breaths. "Unless you have qualms about killing thieves."

"Thieves, not likely. Terrorists like these, none whatsoever. In fact, on my time off, I like to rent a boat and sail along the coast of Somalia and kill would-be hijackers. It's my way of giving back to the world."

Khalid sighed, a burst of static erupting in Tankov's ear. "You're a complicated man, Alexie. Just remember that I'm Muslim."

"A Muslim thief."

"Collector. There's a difference."

"Not in my books, but I'll leave it to your Allah to judge you."

"My Allah is the same as your God."

"I'm an Atheist."

There was a grunt. "That explains a few things. Do you want the job or not?"

"Wire the deposit, and we'll be happy to clean up your mess."

The call ended and Tankov looked at the rest of his team. "We're back in business, boys. Just as I predicted." He rose and stared out the window of their hotel, the Acropolis dominating the view.

Good thing I planned ahead.

Phaleron Delta Necropolis

Athens, Greece

Acton stood beside their SUV, outside the dig site. The police still had it sealed off, and were letting no one inside. The talk last night was that they thought this was just petty criminals biting off more than they could chew, but something had changed, and he was guessing some of the bodies had been identified.

His phone rang and he checked the display, smiling. He showed it to Laura. "It's Hugh." He swiped his thumb, taking the call. "Hey, Hugh, how are you?"

"Are you somewhere you can talk privately?"

Acton looked around at the large number of people. "Not really." He stared at the SUV. "Just a second." He opened the passenger door for Laura. "He wants to talk privately."

Leather stepped over to join them. "Is that Agent Reading?"

Acton nodded, pressing the phone to his ear. "Can Cameron listen in?"

"Yes."

They all climbed inside and Acton started the engine, firing up the air conditioning, the heat already oppressive outside, and even more so inside. The Bluetooth pairing he had set up earlier connected.

"Okay, you're on with me, Laura, and Cameron."

The back door opened and Mai then Tommy hopped in.

"Ahhh, air conditioning," sighed Tommy who paused, noticing everyone was staring at them. "Umm, did we interrupt something?"

"You're also on with Tommy and Mai."

"Fine. Lock your bloody doors."

Acton grinned and pressed the button to comply. "Done."

"Good. First, let me say that you should have told me you were involved in a firefight. I could already be there."

Acton winked at the others. "I figured we should only let you know when something out of the ordinary happens. And with us, well, you know…"

"Uh huh. I *do* know, and that's the problem. Anyway, I can be there late afternoon. It's my day off, and I can probably convince my boss it's official business and stay until this is cleared up."

Laura leaned closer to the microphone. "No, Hugh, you enjoy your day off. If we had known, we wouldn't have sent you anything."

"Don't you ever use my day off as an excuse not to let me know when you've got yourselves knee deep into it once again. Colonel, I assume they're secure?"

Leather leaned in from the back seat. "Relatively. More so than last night. We were still getting established, and I had just arrived. The

142

Greek team I had brought in took heavy casualties, but were able to wipe out half a dozen of the hostiles. Replacements have already arrived, and more are on standby, awaiting a decision on what happens to this location."

"But you think they're safe?"

"For now. I don't think we have to worry about another attack. A few got away, and we don't know if there are more, or if they have the capacity for reinforcements. The site is swarming with police now, so it is protected. We're going to head back to the hotel, right?"

Acton and Laura both nodded.

"Once we get there, they'll be safe."

"Good. If you need me, just let me know."

Laura patted the dash as if it were Reading. "You enjoy your day off and don't worry about us. Plans with Spencer?"

"As a matter of fact, yes. And if I don't leave soon, I'll be late. Oh, before I forget. All but one of those numbers you sent me led to nothing."

"And the one that didn't?" asked Acton.

"A local fence. His name is Karan Damos. Be careful, he's got quite the record, so don't go looking for him. Just let this go, and consider yourselves lucky to have gotten out of this alive."

Acton nodded. "That's our thinking too. We're going to talk things over with Professor Antoniou and see if there's anything we can do to help from a funding perspective, then head back home."

Laura squeezed his thigh. "Maybe we'll drop by and visit with you tonight if you don't mind?"

Acton could almost hear the smile through the phone. "You know you're always welcome."

"Fantastic."

"Wait, just a second."

Acton's eyes narrowed. "What?"

"Michelle just brought me the files on your dead thieves." The start of a whistle was replaced with a burst of static. "Okay, I *definitely* want you guys out of there ASAP."

Acton tensed. "Why?"

"They've all been linked to the Suqut Brigade. It's an offshoot of ISIS that has been hawking a lot of stolen artifacts on the black market. They're vicious, brutal thugs, and won't hesitate to kill. If they're involved, you don't want to be."

That settled things in Acton's mind. "Understood. We'll let you know when we're leaving, and what time the jet will be landing in London."

"Do that. Maybe we'll order Chinese."

Laura smiled. "As long as it's from our favorite place!"

"It's a date."

Acton patted his stomach. "Mmmm, moo shu pork."

Tommy perked up. "I love moo shu!"

Acton looked back at him and Mai. "Umm, you better set two more places for dinner. Tommy and Mai are coming too."

"Ahh, have you seen my flat?"

Acton laughed. "Maybe we'll meet at Laura's. It's bigger."

"Good idea. I'll see you tonight."

The call ended and Acton was about to suggest beating a hasty retreat to the hotel when there was a knock at his window, causing him to flinch.

Calm down!

He lowered the window for Antoniou who peered inside. "Everything okay?"

Acton nodded. "Yes, we were just on a call with our Interpol friend." He gestured at the scene out the front window. "What's the word?"

Antoniou frowned. "They're not letting anyone in today. So, my wife and I would like to take you all to lunch. Our way of apologizing for everything that has happened, and to thank you for your offer to help."

Laura smiled. "Oh, you don't have to do that."

"We insist. Please, let us do this for you."

Acton's stomach rumbled. "Well, I'm starving, so let's do it."

Antoniou beamed. "Splendid. Let me go get her, she'll be so happy."

Antoniou disappeared and Leather opened the rear door. "I'll take my leave now. I want to go over some new security protocols just in case you decide to stay."

Laura shook her head. "Oh, we'll be leaving this afternoon."

Leather smiled. "Ma'am, I know you well enough to always expect the unexpected."

Acton laughed. "Well, just this once you'll be wasting your time. After last night, we're outta here. Guaranteed."

Leather gave a casual salute along with a bemused smile. "Enjoy your lunch."

Acton looked at Laura. "I don't think he believes us."

Laura shrugged. "Would you?" She turned to Leather. "Cameron, do what you must, but spend some time with your friend. I doubt she's too happy being left alone."

Leather frowned. "You might be right." His frown deepened. "This is not the job if you don't want to remain single." He gave them another salute then shut the door.

Laura sighed. "Now I feel terrible."

"You didn't choose his job."

"I know, but I'm the one who has him all over the world, protecting our sites, insisting he be the one that's actually there."

"Well, maybe we should back off on that. All of his men are excellent."

She nodded. "I know. You're right, of course."

"I always am."

She patted his cheek. "Don't get cocky, mister."

He gave a toothy grin. "You're right. I'll save that for—"

"James!" She motioned toward the back seat with her eyes. Acton turned around, facing Tommy and Mai.

"Sorry kids, adult talk, close your ears."

Tommy snickered and Mai held his arm, resting her head on his shoulder. "I sooo want to be like them."

Damos Residence

Athens, Greece

Damos took the final bite of his *moussaka* then put down his fork, leaning back in his chair with a satisfied groan as he swallowed. He smiled appreciatively at his wife.

"Another masterpiece, as usual."

She batted a hand at him. "You say that every meal."

"And I mean it every time." He leaned in and tickled his daughter's stomach, eliciting a squirm and a giggle. "Don't I!"

"Mommy's the best cook ever!"

"And Daddy agrees."

A bang downstairs had his eyes narrowing and his wife staring toward the staircase that led to his shop below. He wiped his mouth with his napkin and rose. "I'll check it out."

His heart hammered when he heard footsteps on the stairs.

Multiple sets.

He took two steps toward the buffet and pulled open one of the drawers, retrieving his gun. He pointed at the bedroom down the hall. "Take her, now. Go out the window if I don't signal you in thirty seconds."

His wife, pale and trembling, grabbed their daughter and rushed down the hall as three men rounded the corner, stepping into the small kitchen.

Damos kept the gun at his side, but it didn't go unnoticed. "What do you want? What is the meaning of this, coming into my home?"

"We're here to discuss what went wrong last night."

His eyes narrowed, then he finally put two and two together when he noticed the thick beards. "You're from the Suqut Brigade."

They all nodded as one, the leader stepping toward the side, staring down the hallway Damos had sent his family. "My boss is not pleased with you. We lost six—"

"Seven," interjected another.

"—men last night. My boss thinks it's your fault."

Damos paled slightly, shaking his head vigorously. "Absolutely not. How could I know they had that extra security? Nobody knew."

"She knew."

Damos' shoulders sagged, realizing he shouldn't have lied to them. "She must have. But I swear, she didn't tell me."

Why stop lying now?

"I don't believe you."

"It's the truth. I swear."

The man took several steps down the hallway. "Perhaps if I asked your wife and daughter. Perhaps they might tell me what I want to know."

Damos' lower lip trembled as he remembered the stories about what ISIS did to women in their so-called Caliphate, and how even the Koran endorsed the sexual enslavement of the women of their enemies. "Please don't hurt them. They're innocent in all of this. They don't even know what I do."

"I find it hard to believe that your lovely wife has no idea how this wonderful food is put on your table." The man rubbed his thumb through the sauce left on Damos' daughter's plate. He sucked it clean, nodding appreciatively. "Your wife is a fine cook. I wonder how she is in the bedroom."

Damos' arm raised swiftly, the gun now mere inches from the man's head. "You won't touch her."

"Perhaps, but you'll never know."

Something hit him hard on the back of the head and he collapsed, his world going black almost instantly.

Please don't touch them!

Oroscopo Restaurant

Athens, Greece

"At least let us pay for Tommy and Mai!"

Antoniou shook his head emphatically. "Absolutely not. I said lunch was on us, and I meant it. Your grad students were always included."

Laura frowned with a sigh. "Very well. But next time lunch is on us."

Antoniou grinned. "I wouldn't have it any other way!"

Acton patted his stomach. "That was a fantastic meal. What were those pastry things called?"

"Spanakopita."

"They should just call it 'crack.' I could eat those all day."

Tommy did the old stretch fake, ending with an arm around Mai who didn't seem to mind. "Me too. When we get back to the States, I'm checking UberEats for a restaurant that has those. Pair those with some samosas, and I'd be in heaven."

Mai's eyes narrowed. "Samosas?"

Tommy eyed her. "You've never had samosas?"

She shrugged. "Never heard of them."

He grinned. "Then you're in for a treat when we get home."

Acton had to agree, and made a mental note to track some down when they returned.

The bill paid, they headed for the exit and stepped into the early afternoon heat, the sun baking down on the concrete jungle surrounding them. Acton groaned. "I never thought I'd say it, but I'm looking forward to London's weather."

Laura patted his chest. "You never did like the heat, did you?"

Acton shook his head. "Why do you think I chose to study the Incans in the mountains of Peru, rather than the Egyptians in the deserts of Africa?"

Laura stared up at the sun, shielding her eyes as she drew in a slow breath. "I love the heat. It's just so unlike England."

Acton eyed her, a bemused smile on her face. "With your fair skin and auburn hair, it's a wonder you don't turn into one big freckle."

She rubbed her face. "Never had that problem, thankfully. Poor Jenny though, she was not made for the sun."

Acton chuckled, thinking of Terrence Mitchell's wife. "She definitely shouldn't have married Terrence, especially now that you've relegated him to the desert for most of the year."

Laura shrugged. "She seems happy."

"She does that."

A van pulled up rather quickly, causing Acton to pause, instinctively stepping in front of Laura. The van doors all opened at once and four armed men, their faces covered by hoods, jumped out. Mai screamed and Acton spread out his arms, ushering Laura, Mai, and Tommy back toward the restaurant entrance as Antoniou and his wife stood frozen.

"Basil! Get back!"

But it was too late. The armed men grabbed Juno by the arms, hauling her toward the van as she screamed, struggling against them. Laura took over, grabbing Tommy and Mai by an arm each and hauling them back through the doors as Acton advanced, reaching for a weapon that wasn't there. He grabbed Antoniou as he began after his wife, hauling him back as two weapons were aimed at them. The doors slammed shut and the van squealed away as Acton raced into the middle of the street after it, trying to read the license plate, but it was of no use. He turned to find Tommy recording the scene like a typical millennial, and pushed him back toward the sidewalk as the others emerged from the safety of the restaurant. He pointed at Laura.

"Call Cameron!"

She nodded and had her phone out moments later as he dialed Reading's number.

I guess we're not leaving today after all.

King George Hotel

Athens, Greece

Leather stared at Adelaide, content. The past two hours had been a lot of fun, beyond the sex. The past hour had just been spent talking, discovering the likes and dislikes of a new lover, the broad strokes of life that had created the person he now shared a bed with.

And hers had been a fascinating life, and she seemed equally enthralled with his own, though much of it was classified and would be a black box to her. She seemed fine with that, her position at the embassy exposing her to the concept of compartmentalization on a regular basis.

It was something his ex-wife could never comprehend.

But Adelaide didn't seem to care about that at all.

"This has been nice."

She smiled at him, running a finger through his chest hair. "Really nice. When can we do it again?"

He sighed. "I'm not sure. Maybe in a month? How long are you in Cairo?"

"For the foreseeable future. I'm stationed there now, so it's not a temporary assignment. How long are you at that dig?"

"That won't be shutting down any time soon. I'll be in and out of there for years, probably. Where I go in between though isn't set in stone."

She grinned. "So, Cairo could be in your future?"

He leaned in and gave her a passionate kiss. "It's a definite possibility."

She sighed, lying back on the pillow, a smile on her face as she closed her eyes. "Can I confess something?"

His stomach flipped. "Umm, sure."

She reached out and blindly took his hand, her eyes still closed, as if she were afraid to look at him. "I think I'm falling for you."

His stomach flipped again and his heart hammered. No one had said anything like that to him since his ex-wife, and he had forgotten how exciting and terrifying it was. He let go of her hand and slid his arm under her neck, rolling her toward him, then hugged her hard. "Me too."

She returned the hug, a sigh of relief escaping at the reciprocated sentiment. It was early, probably too early, yet there was no denying there was something there between them. Nobody had said anything about love, but the intensity between them was unlike anything he had ever experienced, she dominated his thoughts beyond just the sexual, and he genuinely enjoyed talking to her, even though most of those conversations had taken place in a bed.

He couldn't wait to spend more time with her, getting to know her, discovering whether they truly were compatible, whether there truly was a future to be had here. He just prayed his job didn't get in the way once again.

"You realize that what's happened the past couple of days is likely to happen again."

She pushed away from him gently, giving herself space to look at him. "What do you mean? Armed madmen storming a dig site is normal?"

He grunted. "You'd be surprised, though that's not exactly what I meant. What I meant was that my job means I get interrupted. It means plans that are made could easily need to be broken. Like here. I didn't think I'd have to be away so much."

She smiled. "No apology necessary." She leaned closer. "Actually, I think it's kind of sexy." She attacked him, and nothing else was said until they both collapsed beside each other, finally spent.

He smiled at the ceiling. "You make me feel like a young lad again."

She rolled over on her side, facing him. "You mean you did this when you were a boy?"

He chuckled. "Okay, young man."

"That's better. I was beginning to think I'd have to call the police on myself."

He laughed, then frowned, a heavy sigh escaping as his thoughts returned to what he had been saying before he was wonderfully interrupted. He rolled into a cross-legged position. "I have to warn you, right now, that getting involved with me can be unpredictable."

She grinned. "Why, are you a little sick up here?" She tapped his forehead.

He took her hand and held it. "No, I mean my job. I'm the head of security for a *very* wealthy woman, who though very pleasant, is quite demanding when it comes to the safety of her students."

"As she should be. They are, after all, children."

"University students, but yes, they are young. We may not see much of each other."

She smiled and pushed him onto his back, climbing on top of him. "Then how about we just focus on the sex?"

A Cheshire grin spread across his face when his phone vibrated on the nightstand. He reached over and checked the display. "See?" He held it up for her, the phone showing a photo of Laura. "Told you." He swiped his thumb. "Hello?"

"Cameron, Juno has been kidnapped at gunpoint. We need you."

He became all business, gently pushing Adelaide off him as he left the bed, his eyes roaming the room for his clothes. "Are you in immediate danger?"

"No, I don't think so. They're gone."

"Was anyone hurt?"

"No."

"Then get inside a public building. Bank or government. Something with lots of people. Send me your location as soon as you're secure. I'm heading out now."

"Okay. I'll send you the location right away."

The call ended and he turned to Adelaide to find her deliciously naked, collecting his clothes and placing them on the bed. He smiled. "Have I told you that you're the best?"

"I am, and no, you haven't."

He gave her a quick peck as he grabbed his underwear. "I'm pretty sure I told you last night."

"That was sex. You always tell your partner they're the best you ever had, even if it isn't true."

"But in both our cases it is, of course."

She grinned. "Of course." She handed him his Kevlar vest. "So, what's going on?"

"The professor's wife has been kidnapped."

She froze for a moment. "Professor Palmer?"

He shook his head. "No, Juno, the Greek professor." He finished stuffing his pockets with the accouterments of the trade, then gave her a quick hug.

"You're right, life with you will be interesting."

He smiled at her. "Will?"

She pushed him away, wagging a finger. "Don't read too much into things." She winked at him. "But I do like interesting."

Athens, Greece

"What are you doing? Why did you take me?"

Rafiq smacked the woman with the back of his hand, turning her cries of protests into less annoying whimpers. "Keep your mouth shut, woman!"

She wiped away a trickle of blood from her lip with the back of her hand before it was grabbed, along with the other, and bound with zip ties by Zaman. "Please, my husband is a professor. He's not a rich man. We have no money."

"I said, shut up!" He raised his hand, but she cowered before him, his dominance established. He shoved a rag into her mouth, then jabbed a finger into her chest. "If you know what's good for you, you won't say another word, or your husband will be getting you back in pieces." He squeezed one of her breasts. "But not before we have our fun with you, kafir."

Her eyes widened with horror and fear, and his mind flashed back to the sex slave he had been honored with for several months back in the Caliphate. It had been an incredible time. He had never understood until then, the pleasures that came with complete and total control over a sexual partner. The Koran in Sura 4:24 said, "And all married women are forbidden unto you save those whom your right hands possess," and he was merely following the word of Allah, which made it all the more wonderful. During those days of bliss, he often wondered if Jannah was like that. Seventy-two virgins, under his complete control and dominance for eternity.

I can't wait to get there.

And the way his man was driving, that might be sooner than planned.

"Slow down, there's no one following us."

"Sorry."

He stared at his prisoner, trembling in the corner, and sneered. "You're mistaken about your husband."

She stared at him, her eyes suggesting confusion.

"He has something I want. Which makes him a very wealthy man."

She shook her head, shouting something into the rag, something he couldn't care less to understand. For before this night was over, he would either have what he wanted, or he'd have her.

Either way, he'd be satisfied.

Though both would be better.

The Red Lion Pub

London, England

Reading drained the last of his pint, calling for another, as his son Spencer failed to keep up.

"I didn't know you could drink a beer that fast."

Reading tapped the table. "Decades of practice, lad. One day, you'll be tossing one back and impressing my grandson."

"What if it's a granddaughter?"

Reading paused. "I don't know how to impress a daughter."

Spencer grinned. "Then good thing you had a son."

Reading laughed, smiling at the barmaid as she delivered his fresh pint. "I'm glad we're doing this."

Spencer nodded, wiping his upper lip free of the froth from his last large gulp. "Me too. I'm sorry I wasted so many years."

Reading shook his head. "You were just a boy. It wasn't your fault."

"Yeah, well, mother kind of had a hand in that too."

"We'll not speak ill of your mother."

Spencer stared at the bottom of his glass. "Sorry."

Reading leaned closer. "Even if you're telling the truth." He patted him on the arm then leaned back. "I'm proud of you, son. You're making something of yourself. From what I've been told, you're doing extremely well at Hendon."

Spencer eyed him. "Have you been checking up on me?"

"Absolutely."

Spencer wagged a finger. "Don't interfere."

"Wouldn't dream of it. And from what I've been told, there's no need to check up on you anymore. But if you ever need help, you let me know. Your old man has a lot of connections still. Even at the police college."

"I want to do this on my own."

"I wouldn't have it any other way. You don't need my help, you'll do just fine." Reading sighed. "My son, a copper. Fantastic!"

"Did you ever think you'd see the day?"

Reading roared with laughter, raising his glass. "If you had told me a year ago that my son would be at Hendon Police College, I would have called you barmy!"

His phone vibrated beside his glass and he leaned over to see Acton's smiling mug on display. "Uh oh."

"What?"

"Jim." He swept his thumb across the display. "Hello?"

"Juno's been kidnapped!"

Reading's eyebrows shot up and he pressed the phone harder against his ear, a pub not the best place for important conversations. "Are you safe?"

"Yes, I think so. We're heading into a bank right now."

"Has someone called the police yet?"

"I think some bystanders did. I hear sirens now. Laura is on the phone with Cameron right now."

Reading cursed. "He's not with you?"

"No, he's at the hotel."

"What the bloody hell good is private security if they're not with you?"

"We all thought it was over. It was just lunch, then we were getting on the plane."

Reading shook his head. "Never mind all that. Secure yourself, then call me back. I'll head to the office now and make arrangements to join you."

"Use the account."

Reading frowned, always hating accessing the private account his friends had set up for him in case of emergencies. But this was one of those times it truly was an emergency. "I will."

"And don't skimp. Do whatever it takes to get here as fast as you can."

"Just secure yourself, then call me back."

"Okay, talk to you soon."

Reading ended the call, pushing his beer aside. "I really hate to do this. We just got here, and the match hasn't even started yet."

Spencer chuckled. "With friends like yours, it's a wonder that you can ever keep an appointment."

Reading grunted. "You have no idea. Are you okay?"

Spencer nodded. "You're a cop. Your friends need you. You wouldn't be the dad I know if you didn't go help them."

Reading smiled. "You're a good son."

"And you're a good dad. I, umm, know we had our problems, but I like to think everything is good between us now."

Reading's chest ached at the words. "So do I."

"Now, go to Greece before people start crying."

Reading laughed. "You are *definitely* my son." He rose, as did his son, and they exchanged a thumping hug. "I'll see you when I get back."

"Be careful."

Reading left the pub with mixed emotions, worried about his friends, but pleased things were going so well with his son after so many years estranged. Spencer was a changed man, and was finally making something of himself.

And there wasn't a prouder father in all of London.

Life is good.

Alpha Bank
Athens, Greece

Acton stood with the others near the rear of the bank, a quick explanation from Antoniou as to what was going on garnering action from a sympathetic manager. Through the glass doors, they could see half a dozen police cars, and at least a couple of dozen officers, securing the area, but he wasn't going out there.

Not yet.

His phone vibrated with the call he had been waiting for.

Leather.

He answered. "Cameron?"

"Where are you?"

Acton spotted the man striding through the doors. "We're in the back." He gestured toward the manager standing nearby as Leather was challenged by the on-edge guards. "He's with us."

Something was shouted and Leather was let through. Acton and the others rushed out to join him.

"Is everyone okay?"

"They took my wife!"

Leather ignored the Greek professor, instead giving the once over to the people he was responsible for. "I want you to stay in here. I'm going to go outside and find out who's in charge, then we'll go from there. Expect this to be a long day. There will be a lot of questions, especially after last night."

Acton sighed. "We know. But our first priority has to be Juno."

Leather agreed. "Of course. But that's a police matter." He held up a hand, cutting off any protests. "Let me go find out what's going on, okay?"

Acton nodded. "You're right, of course."

Leather excused himself then left the bank, crossing the street. Within minutes, he returned with two uniformed officers and a man in a suit who, from the arrogant bearing, Acton presumed was the one in charge.

"I am Major Nicolo of the Hellenic Police. I'll need you all to come to the station so you can be properly interrogated."

Acton's eyes narrowed. "You think we had something to do with this?"

Nicolo regarded him for a moment. "Absolutely. You may not be aware, but I've taken over the investigation of what happened last night. You four"—he pointed at Acton, Laura, Tommy, and Mai—"arrive, and within hours we have seven dead, another half-dozen wounded, and now Professor Galanos is kidnapped in broad daylight. I think this has everything to do with you. I don't know what you're up to, but I intend to find out."

Acton bit his tongue, and was about to lose the battle when his phone vibrated in his hand.

"Don't answer that."

Acton checked the display. It was Reading. He stared at Nicolo. "I'm an American citizen and I'm taking this call." He swiped his thumb. "Hugh, I think we're all about to be arrested."

"What? By who?"

"Greek police. A Major..." Acton looked at the man.

"Nicolo."

"Nicolo. He thinks Laura and I are behind the attack last night and the kidnapping."

"Is he daft? Put him on the phone!"

Acton held out the phone for Nicolo. "Agent Reading from Interpol wants to talk with you."

Nicolo's eyes bulged slightly and he took the phone, walking away from them, no doubt to keep them from hearing what he was expecting to be an unpleasant call. The discussion was clearly heated, the odd stray word reaching Acton's ear, but after a few minutes, a more contrite Nicolo returned, handing back the phone.

"It would appear I may have been, umm, mistaken."

Acton nodded, noting the call was still connected. "Hugh?"

"Hopefully I'll get there before you two get tossed in prison."

"Call Laura's agent. She'll arrange a private jet. That'll be the quickest way to get here."

"You know I hate doing that."

"Do it."

A heavy sigh burst through the speaker. "Fine. If I ever win the lottery, all flights are on me."

Acton grinned. "Have you been buying tickets?"

"Nope."

"I hear it improves the odds."

"Sod off. I'll see you this evening."

The call ended and Acton pocketed his phone, returning his attention to the slightly calmer major. "Now that that is straightened out, we need to figure out who is behind this."

Tommy cleared his throat. "Umm, I got a photo of the van. Do you want the license plate number?"

Everyone turned toward the young man, Acton replaying the events of earlier, remembering how Tommy had been on the street with him, rather than inside the restaurant as he had thought. "You got a photo?"

"I got video."

"How?"

He grinned. "I'm a millennial. We don't run from danger, we run toward it with our phones so we can go viral on social media."

Acton chuckled, silently apologizing for cursing the generation earlier.

Kids.

Nicolo had apparently had enough with the delays. "Will you, as *witnesses*, please come to the station with me for formal statements?"

Acton decided to have some fun. "I thought you'd never ask."

Outside the Damos Residence

Athens, Greece

Utkin lowered his binoculars, glancing at Tankov. "Good idea watching him."

Tankov grunted as they watched the fence, Damos, stuffed into the back of a car, clearly against his will. "I do have one occasionally."

Utkin chuckled as he started the engine. "Occasionally." He jabbed a thumb in Tankov's direction. "That new face wasn't one of them."

Tankov lowered his binoculars, running a hand over his plastic surgeon's latest creation as Utkin followed their target. "I thought it looked pretty good."

"Do you even remember what you looked like before we got into this business?"

Tankov grunted. He had to admit sometimes he wasn't sure who stared back at him in the mirror anymore. Sometimes he'd catch a reflection in a store window, or the rearview mirror, and it would startle him, giving him a strange out of body experience that was more disturbing than anything else.

But it was his chosen method of staying anonymous. If his identity was revealed on a job, he had his face redone. It was simple, and a lot more convenient than constantly living in hiding. The only time it ever concerned him was when he visited his mother.

She cried every time, inevitably bringing out the photo album. "You looked like your father! Why would you do this?"

He dared not tell her the truth, instead telling her it was a necessity from his days in Spetsnaz. *That* she could accept, her belief system rooted in the old Soviet one—she understood sacrificing for the state. If she knew the truth, that he was an international art thief, wanted by pretty much every police force in the world, it would break her heart.

And he could never have that.

He pointed at the vehicle. "Let's forget about my face, and worry about where they're headed."

Utkin nodded. "And about why they took him."

Tankov agreed. "I don't think they have it."

"Why?"

"Why kidnap the fence? If they had it, they'd just deliver it and move on, or keep it for themselves, and move on. Either way, the fence is no longer of any value. He's just the guy who made the introductions. Even if they wanted to sell it, he wouldn't be the one you went to. He's small-time."

"So then why?"

"Well, if they don't have it, then they must be thinking he might know who does."

"He double-crossed them?"

"Possibly. He's a colossal idiot if he did. You don't cross people like this."

Utkin frowned. "Didn't our intel report on him say he had a wife and kid?"

Tankov nodded. "Maybe an anonymous call to the police is in order."

"Maybe."

Tankov arranged it as they continued to tail the kidnapped Damos, and were soon in a residential neighborhood of questionable pedigree. He smiled as the car parked and the doors opened. "Looks like we're here."

Utkin drove past them, finding a spot farther down the street. "Lovely neighborhood."

Tankov had to agree it wasn't somewhere he'd want to live, but it was exactly the type of place where nobody would pay attention to anything their neighbors did. "Call in the team. I want the area scouted, and cameras in that house. We need to see what we're facing."

Suqut Brigade Safe House

Athens, Greece

Rafiq took a long swig from his bottle of water, satisfied with jobs well done. Damos had been taken without incident, as had the professor's wife. And if all continued to go well, he'd have what he wanted before the end of the day, then he could leave this wretched city teeming with decadence.

He hated Europe, and looked forward to the day the flag of Islam flew over every capital. It was inevitable. The West kept inviting Muslims in, and Muslims had babies at twice the pace. Demographics assured victory.

Then, and only then, would he feel comfortable in these cities that had given birth to the people who caused him so much pain.

And to win the ultimate victory, to establish the worldwide caliphate, they needed money. And this artifact, once retrieved and handed over to the sheik, would give them a hefty sum for a couple of days work, allowing the cause to buy weapons and ammunition to continue the fight. For though the West thought they had been victorious, all they had done was disperse the members of ISIS throughout the region, and their own homelands.

Pathetic.

The moronic leadership of the West were so obsessed with political correctness, that they were allowing their own citizens, who had gone and fought *for* ISIS, to return, and in some countries, with little to no consequences. At least he could respect England and France. They were actively killing their own citizens before they returned, because they knew once they did, there was nothing they could do without the Social Justice Warriors taking up the cause of forgiving those who had betrayed their own countries.

He loved it.

He just prayed that he'd see the day when Islam ruled all.

Maybe I'll move to Belgium.

In less than twenty years, it was predicted Brussels would be majority Muslim. The moment it happened, faithful Muslims would elect a new government, establish Sharia law, and drive out the Christians that remained. Brussels would be the first major Western city to fall.

The first of many.

And to hasten the cause, he needed money. And for that, he needed information.

And leverage.

Which he now had.

He pointed at Zaman. "Get some video of her, but keep her gagged. I don't want her revealing anything that might lead them to us. We'll send it to the husband with our demands. I want this over with as quickly as possible. This is way too much heat."

Zaman rose, pulling out his phone. "As soon as women are involved, the police get *too* involved."

"Exactly. Some ancient artifacts, most don't care. Female flesh, everything changes." He drew his knife from his belt and headed to the room holding Damos. He smiled at the terrified man, his eyes widening with fear as he spotted the blade. "I think we need to have a talk."

Outside the Suqut Brigade Safe House
Athens, Greece

Utkin expertly guided the small drone as Tankov watched in the back of their state of the art van that had arrived just hours ago by transport from a storage facility in Germany. That was one of the lovely things about Europe. It covered such a tiny area geographically, pretty much anything could be delivered overland within less than a day, with no internal borders.

He loved Europe.

When he retired, if he ever survived long enough to do so, he could picture himself settling somewhere on the Mediterranean. Sun, surf, yachts, women, food, alcohol. Not necessarily in that order.

Perhaps it's time.

But it was the thrill he'd miss. Here he was, working with incredible equipment, illegally armed to the teeth, collecting intel on a terrorist cell that they were going to slaughter, perhaps in a matter of hours.

Good fun.

Something not found on a beach or in a bed.

"Deploying now." Utkin pressed a button and the camera from the drone showed a small device impale itself on a window. Utkin checked something on the computer. "We've got a good signal." An image appeared on one of the screens showing a woman with her back to the camera, tied to a chair. "Repositioning for the next camera."

Tankov stared at the one image they had, trying to spot any of their enemy, as Utkin launched the second camera, the tiny devices able to transmit video, as well as sound that it picked up as vibrations of the glass.

I love the tech.

The second camera went live, the fence, Damos, visible from the side, his face bloodied, his shirt heavily stained.

"Somebody did a number on him."

Utkin glanced at the image and nodded. "We might be doing him a favor if we killed him along with the others."

Tankov shook his head. "Not our target."

Utkin deployed the third camera, the image appearing as a black screen.

"What's going on?"

Utkin pulled the drone back and frowned. "They've closed the curtains, but you can hear them, they're still in that room."

"That will have to do. Start monitoring. I want to know what they're up to, and how many there are. And we need to confirm they don't have the artifact."

Utkin leaned back in his chair. "This reminds me of Chechnya."

Tankov chuckled. "It does, doesn't it? But there, we'd just go in and kill them all once we knew what was what."

Utkin sighed. "I miss the old days sometimes."

"But not the paycheck."

Utkin laughed. "I have more loose change in my couch than I ever made working for Mother Russia."

Tankov grunted. "Sad but true." He held up a finger. "They're talking. Are you recording this?"

"Yup."

"Good. Let's see if they can do our job for us."

King George Hotel
Athens, Greece

Laura flopped onto the couch of their suite, Acton dropping beside her as Tommy, Mai, and Antoniou occupied other seats while Leather made a quick check of the several rooms.

"I guess dinner with Hugh is off."

Acton stared at Laura for a moment. "Oh, did I forget to tell you? He's on his way." He checked his watch. "In fact, he should be here any minute."

Laura sighed, rubbing her eyes with her knuckles. "No, you didn't forget, I did. Wait!" She checked her watch. "Are you kidding me? We spent five hours there? He might as well have arrested us. What a wasted day! We could have been doing something useful!"

"Helping find my wife isn't useful?"

Laura's cheeks flushed at Antoniou's words, words Acton bristled at as they were uncalled for. "Oh, God, that's not what I meant! I meant we could have been doing something useful to find her."

Antoniou waved a hand at her, dismissing the apology. "I'm sorry, I'm just so worried. But what can we possibly do that the police couldn't?"

Acton grinned. "You'd be surprised." He turned to Tommy. "Can you work your magic?"

Tommy was already attacking the computer in his lap, Acton always amazed at how fast he could work a machine. "Way ahead of you. I'm pulling the traffic camera footage now."

Antoniou's eyes narrowed. "How?"

Acton explained, letting the young man continue to work. "Let's just say Tommy wasn't always, umm, on the right side of the law?"

Tommy blushed and Mai flushed, the young woman apparently a little excited at the notion.

Likes the bad boys?

Antoniou shook his head. "I don't understand."

Tommy looked up from his keyboard. "I used to be a hacker. Not one of the good ones. I got busted and went straight." He grinned. "Now I only break the law for the professor."

Acton laughed and Tommy went back to work. "If he can access the cameras, we might be able to track where the van went. Then we can tell the police, and they can rescue your wife."

"But wouldn't the police be doing that?"

"I'm sure they will. But they might need to wait for permission, warrants, who knows." Acton nodded toward Tommy. "And he's the best I've ever seen at this."

"I'm in."

Acton grinned. "See?"

Everyone gathered around the laptop and watched video showing the kidnapping. Tommy started working the system, following the van, then stopped.

"Umm, this is going to take a while, and nobody's brushed their teeth since lunch."

Everybody backed off, hands covering mouths.

A knock at the door had Leather checking the peephole. "It's Agent Reading." He opened the door and their friend from Interpol entered, concern on his face. He slapped Leather on the back.

"Thank God you're here, Cameron."

"Likewise." Leather turned to Laura. "Ma'am, if it's okay, I'd like to bring Miss Burnett up here, just so we're all in one location."

"Absolutely, of course."

Leather bowed his head then left. Reading locked the door then joined them, Laura introducing him to Antoniou.

"Have you heard anything?" asked Acton as their friend sat.

Reading shook his head. "Nothing new that's of use. They haven't found the vehicle used in the kidnapping, and they have no idea who is involved, though I think it's probably safe to say it's the same group as last night."

Laura frowned. "The Suqut Brigade."

"Exactly. The question is, why? They have what they wanted, so why take her?"

Acton leaned back in his chair. "The only thing I've been able to think of is that they're going to use her to authenticate the artifact to whoever the buyer is. That's why those Russians kept Laura."

Laura nodded. "And once I did my part, they let me go. Perhaps they'll do the same?"

Reading shook his head. "I wouldn't count on it. Not with these guys." Antoniou paled, and Acton could tell Reading regretted his delivery, though not his words. "I'm sorry, Professor, but I think you deserve the truth. The Russians were businessmen, and because they apparently had a habit of changing their faces as needed, weren't concerned with Laura surviving. But the Suqut Brigade are fanatics, and they hate everything about us, especially empowered women like your wife. When they're done with her, we have to expect that they'll kill her. That means we have to do everything we can to find her before she's no longer of use to them."

Tommy muttered a curse.

Acton's eyes narrowed. "What?"

"I lost them." He threw up his hands. "Half the damned cameras in this city aren't working. I think they must have changed vehicles in a blind spot. There's no way I'm going to find them."

Antoniou held his face in his hands as he bent forward. "Then what are we going to do?" He leaped to his feet, an accusatory finger stabbing out at everyone there. "I thought you said you could help!" He spun, heading toward the door, Acton about to stop him when the man turned back and stopped. "This is all my fault!"

Laura rose, stepping toward him and putting an arm over his shoulders. "Of course it's not."

"It is. We should have given up long ago, but my pigheadedness wouldn't allow it. We're broke! Absolutely broke! That lunch today? That was for show. We'll barely be able to eat for the next two weeks because of it, and it's all my fault. I've poured every cent we have into this project, despite her objections." He dropped into the nearest chair, tears streaming down his cheeks. "She's been wonderful. She's done everything she can to cut our expenses. She's begged and borrowed from friends and family, and worked the Internet for donations." He squeezed the bridge of his nose, his eyes tightly closed. "She's my rock," he gasped. "I don't know what I'd do without her. If anything happens…"

Laura patted his shoulder. "We'll do everything we can." She looked at Tommy. "Is there anything more you can do?"

He made a show of cracking his fingers. "Never give up! Never surrender!"

Suqut Brigade Safe House

Athens, Greece

"Give me your husband's phone number."

"Why?"

Rafiq pressed a knife against the woman's throat. "The number, now!"

"But he doesn't—"

He slipped the knife through the buttons on her shirt and tucked the blade under one of her breasts. "If anything but a number comes out of your mouth next, I cut it off."

He felt her tremble under his power, under his control, and it excited him. He leered at her, determined now more than ever to have this woman before his business with her was done.

He might even take her with him.

A white woman with a broken spirit would fetch a lot of money on the black market. He had no doubt there were many sheiks out there who would pay handsomely for such a prize.

But not before he had broken her of any will to resist.

She gave him the number, thankfully preserving her value with two breasts, then he shoved the gag back in her mouth. He left her, whimpering, and returned to join the others. He dropped into his chair and motioned toward Zaman, on the phone with their lookout.

"Are they at the hotel?"

Zaman nodded. "Yeah, they just arrived."

"Police?"

"None."

Rafiq smiled. "Good." He pulled up the video recorded of the professor's wife earlier, then forwarded it to the phone number she had just given him. Along with a simple text.

You know what we want.

King George Hotel

Athens, Greece

Tommy jerked back in his chair, frustration on his face, causing the entire room to stop their conversation and focus on him.

"That doesn't look promising."

Tommy frowned at Acton. "I'm sorry, I tried, but all I can be sure of is that the van enters this dead zone, then never comes out. There are half a dozen ways to come out of there, including the way they came in, but I can't find it."

Acton pursed his lips. "So, they switched vehicles. And probably knew about the dead zone."

Tommy nodded. "Right. And they'd have to switch into something similar in size, since there were at least four of them, plus Professor Galanos. But I've gone through the video, and there are literally dozens of vehicles coming out of that area that could fit the bill." His shoulders slumped in defeat. "There are just too many variables. We need a new piece of information that I can use to narrow it down."

Reading checked his phone. "Still nothing from London. I'm going to assume the Greek authorities are canvassing the area for witnesses to any vehicle exchange you're referring to. I'm sure the major will have already found the van and be going over it with a fine-toothed comb. If we're lucky, they'll find something that can help us."

Antoniou sighed. "Luck. It always comes down to luck." His phone vibrated in his hand and he checked the display, his eyes narrowing before his jaw dropped. "I-I think it's them!"

Everyone leaned closer. "What's it say?"

"You know what we want." Antoniou looked at the others. "What do they mean by that? What *do* they want? Why don't they just say it!"

Tommy pointed over his shoulder. "There's a video attached."

Antoniou handed him the phone. "I don't understand these things."

Tommy tapped away at the device then his laptop, and within moments, they were all watching the video. Acton's stomach flipped at the sight of the bruised and battered Juno, tied to a chair, her cheeks stained with tears, her mouth stuffed with a gag.

And terror in her bloodshot eyes.

Ten seconds later it was over, with nothing revealed, nothing said, nothing beyond the text message that had accompanied it.

You know what we want.

Acton returned to his seat. "They have to be talking about the urn. That's the only thing truly of value to anyone outside the academic community, right?"

Antoniou wiped the tears from his face. "Yes, but they have it." He pulled at his hair. "What else could they possibly be talking about?

What else could I have that they want? Money? I'll send them the bank statements. I'm broke! They can have my house, my car, anything!"

"This isn't about money."

Acton looked at Reading. "You sound certain."

Reading smiled. "I've been in this business a tad longer than you lot." He pointed at the phone. "The message tells us a fair bit. If they wanted money, they would have said so, but they don't. They want some object, or some service. This isn't a ransom demand looking for cash, and what could anyone possibly want from an archaeology professor?" He looked at the three of them in the room. "No offense meant."

Acton grinned. "None taken, I'm sure. But if we assume you're right, and it's not money, and it's not some service, then it must be an artifact they're after. Which brings us back to the elephant in the room—they already have the only thing that was worth anything."

"You're forgetting. There's one other clue in that message."

Acton's eyes narrowed, wondering what he could have missed in those five little words. "Enlighten me."

"Our theory was that they might have taken her to validate the artifact to the buyer."

Acton exhaled slowly, his head bobbing. "Which, if true, would mean they'd have no reason to contact anyone. They'd just take her to the meet, then either kill her or release her."

Reading nodded. "Exactly. So, I think we can now safely eliminate that theory. Which brings us back to them wanting something from you, Professor. Are you positive there's nothing else of value?"

Antoniou shrugged. "Nothing from a monetary perspective. Some private collectors, I'm sure, would pay dearly to have some genuine artifacts from that era, but we're talking thousands of Euros at best, not millions. And besides, it would be illegal to possess them."

Reading gave Acton a quick look over the naïve statement. "Professor, things have been disappearing for months. Obviously, they're of value to someone, and those people are not concerned with the legalities."

Antoniou sighed, shaking his head. "You're right, of course. But who would be willing to kidnap for such items? *Kill* for such items?"

Acton had to agree. There was no way anyone would kill for a clay jar or a bronze dagger. The monetary value just wasn't there, nor were the bragging rights.

But an urn, inscribed by Cylon himself, with a mystery inside?

That was something someone might kill for.

"It has to be the urn," said Acton.

"But—"

Acton held up his hand, cutting off Antoniou. "Think about it. The urn is the only thing worth any amount of money that could be worth killing for. We're quite certain that the men who kidnapped your wife are the same ones who attacked the dig last night. The only reason they'd attack was to get that urn, but their attack was thwarted."

"But they got the urn!"

Acton shook his head. "No. *Someone* got the urn. Remember, you've had thefts for weeks now."

"Months."

"Okay, months. Hugh, would a group like the Suqut Brigade be the type that would sit around for months, stealing one artifact after another, then fencing them for a few thousand Euros at a time?"

"Absolutely not."

"Exactly." Acton turned to Antoniou. "I think whoever has been stealing your artifacts is someone on the inside."

Antoniou nodded. "Which is what we suspected."

"Right. And I think they took the opportunity to steal the urn while the attack was underway. It's the only thing that fits."

Antoniou sighed. "I can't think of any other possibility either."

"Neither can I. But there's one little problem with this."

Antoniou stared at Acton. "What?"

"The Suqut Brigade obviously thinks *you* are the inside man."

Suqut Brigade Safe House
Athens, Greece

It had been fifteen minutes, and Rafiq was growing impatient. Scratch that. He was already beyond impatient. He stared at the phone again, his mind playing tricks on him, certain he had sensed a vibration that was never there.

Zaman cleared his throat. "Umm, do we know if he got the message?"

Rafiq twisted his beard around his finger. "If it didn't go through, the phone would have said so. It went through, though we don't know if he's actually seen it."

"Then what are we going to do? They must know that we have no way of knowing, so maybe they'll just ignore us and play dumb."

The very notion had Rafiq on his feet, rage building. "Come with me." He stormed down the hall, Zaman on his heels, and entered the woman's room. He handed the phone to Zaman. "Record me."

Zaman tapped the screen a few times, then held the phone out in front of him. Rafiq advanced on the woman, her eyes bulging with fear, and he punched her as hard as he could in the nose, the satisfying crunch of it breaking felt deep in his loins as the endorphins surged through his body—exactly as he imagined every moment of Jannah to be.

The woman cried out against her gag, tears and blood flowing down her cheeks as Rafiq stepped away, indicating for Zaman to get a closeup of her shattered face. Zaman nodded at him, the shot confirmed.

Rafiq grabbed the phone then forwarded the video with another text message.

I'm growing impatient. If you don't respond, we'll show you what we do to infidel women.

King George Hotel
Athens, Greece

"Oh no!"

Acton wrapped his arm around Laura, holding her tight as they all watched in horror the short video showing someone punching Juno in the face, and the resulting damage.

Tommy, his voice cracking, read the message. "It says, 'I'm growing impatient. If you don't respond, we'll show you what we do to infidel women.'"

Antoniou's head lolled to the side, Reading and Acton springing to his aid. Acton turned to Mai. "Get a facecloth from the bathroom and run it under cold water. Tommy, go get some ice."

Mai rushed for the bathroom, but the newly returned Leather stopped Tommy. "I'll get the ice." He left the room, Reading locking the door behind him then holding up a hand, ending Adelaide's attempt to follow.

"Let's all just stay put."

She nodded, returning to her seat as Mai returned with the cold cloth. Acton placed it on the shocked husband's forehead, then gently slapped the man's cheek.

"Basil, can you hear me? Just breathe. You'll be okay, just breathe."

Antoniou moaned then his eyes fluttered open and he inhaled deeply. "Wh-what happened?"

"You fainted." Acton removed the cloth from the man's forehead and placed it in his hand. Antoniou dabbed it against his cheeks and neck as Laura arrived with a glass of water. "Here, drink this."

Antoniou took the water then several healthy gulps, color returning to his cheeks. "I-I don't think I've ever done that before." He smiled weakly. "Don't tell my students. I'll lose any respect I might have with them."

Acton chuckled, happy to see a hint of the sense of humor he knew the man possessed. "Your secret is safe with us." He glanced over his shoulder at the knock at the door, Reading opening it and letting Leather back in. Ice was added to the drink, and a few cubes wrapped in the damp cloth, everyone backing off to give Antoniou some space and some dignity.

Antoniou finally sighed, his old self once again. He pointed at the phone. "We have to reply."

Laura frowned. "Yes, but with what?"

Acton pursed his lips, looking about the room. "The truth?"

Antoniou leaned forward. "But if they find out I don't have it, then they might think Juno's of no value. They might kill her."

Reading nodded. "Then we have to delay them. At least until we can find out where they're holding her." He turned to Tommy.

"Any luck?"

Tommy shook his head. "No." His eyes widened as he stared at Antoniou's phone. "Maybe we can trace the messages!"

Acton's eyes narrowed. "Would they be that stupid?"

"Maybe. We didn't get the message until we arrived. We were at the police station for almost five hours. How did they know to wait just the right amount of time?"

Acton bolted upright. "They know we're here, and not with the police!"

Reading and Leather both sprang into action, Leather checking the hallway then relocking the door, Reading looking out the windows then drawing the blinds. Laura frowned.

"Do you think we're in danger?"

"It's possible."

"I'll call for help." Leather dialed his phone and retreated to the bedroom, calling, Acton assumed, the Greek security team, reemerging moments later. "We'll have a team here in less than fifteen minutes."

Acton pointed at Antoniou's phone. "Before Tommy does anything with that phone, we need to respond before they hurt Juno again."

Laura shook her head. "Do we arrange an exchange?"

Antoniou stared at her. "And when we show up with nothing? What then?"

Acton chewed his cheek for a moment. "We cross that bridge when we get to it."

Reading agreed. "We need to delay the meeting. They'll keep her alive for as long as they think you'll give them what they want."

Antoniou paled slightly. "But won't they want it right away?"

Reading's fingers drummed on his chin for a moment. "Tell them that it is hidden, and the place is being watched by the police. You can't get it until they leave."

Antoniou nodded, picking up the phone, his fingers trembling as he operated the touchscreen. Acton held out his hand.

"Let me."

Antoniou handed him the phone and Acton quickly sent the message then looked at the others. "Done. Now we wait."

Tommy held out his hand. "Gimme. We might not have much time."

Suqut Brigade Safe House
Athens, Greece

A string of expletives erupted from Zaman's mouth as he read the reply to their messages, and though blasphemous, Rafiq was willing to forgive him, as his own had been worse.

"He's playing us. He has to be."

Rafiq tugged at his beard, pacing the small room. "Is he? He says the place he's hidden it is being watched."

Zaman spat. "That's garbage. Watched by who?"

"The police, obviously."

"But why would they be watching where he's hidden it? If they know where it is, then why not just go in and get it?"

Rafiq paused, then sat, wagging a finger. "Maybe that's it. Maybe he's hidden it at his home, and the police are watching the home."

Zaman's jaw dropped slowly as he leaned back in his chair. "Now *that* makes sense. He steals it, hides it at his house. The police have no need to search it, but after we took his wife, they're watching it just in case we show up."

Rafiq stood. "Makes perfect sense to me. Do we know where he lives?"

Zaman shook his head.

Rafiq grabbed a pen and paper from the table, then headed for the woman's room. He tore the rag out of her mouth. "Your home address. Now!"

"Wh-why?"

He smacked her across the face, hard, eliciting a gasped cry and a fresh stream of blood from her shattered nose. "No questions. The address, now."

She gave it to him and he wrote it down.

"Please, what's this all about?"

"Your husband has something we want."

"What?"

"The urn inscribed by Cylon."

Her eyes widened as he shoved the gag back in her mouth, ignoring her denials.

We'll know soon enough.

King George Hotel
Athens, Greece

As the conversation raged over Acton's suggestion the kidnappers thought Antoniou was the thief, Mai flipped through the dozens upon dozens of photos she had taken while at the site. The entire experience had been so fascinating, she had wanted to capture every moment, every sight, so she would never forget it.

And she hoped the images might help her piece together what had happened.

When the attack had occurred, it was late, so most of those working there had already gone home for the day. When the shooting started, she and Tommy had been with the professors, all four of them, in the dig site with Leather and some remaining grad students. From what she could remember, and from what she could see in the photos she had been taking of the just revealed urn, there were no guards in sight, meaning the local security, and Leather's hired security, were all outside of the massive pit that was the dig site.

When the shooting started, Acton had ushered her and Tommy under a tarp, and in the moments before when she could still see, she was pretty sure everybody had headed for the ramp leading out of the dig, though she couldn't be certain.

But what had happened to the two grad students?

She turned to Tommy, still working away. "Do you remember the two grad students?"

Tommy stopped and looked at her. "Huh?"

"The two grad students. The guy and the girl. The ones who joked that they were the Greek versions of us."

Tommy nodded. "Oh yeah, whatever." He grinned at her. "I'm way more handsome than him, and you're ten times as hot as she is."

Mai's cheeks flushed and a tingling sensation surged through her body. If they were alone in the room, she would have mounted him right then and there. "Well, umm, what happened to them?"

Tommy's eyes narrowed. "What do you mean?"

"I mean, when the shooting happened. Where did they go?"

Tommy chewed his cheek for a moment, then his eyebrows popped. "The dude was screaming like a little girl. At first, I thought it was her, but it wasn't."

"And what about her?"

He thought for a moment, then shook his head. "I don't know. I don't remember."

Mai sighed. "Neither do I." She flipped through some photos of the aftermath, then paused on one showing the parking lot, and the female grad student emerging from between the cars. She showed it to Tommy. "Why would she be up here?"

Tommy glanced at the photo. "Is that the parking lot?"

"Yes."

His eyes narrowed. "Did she go up with the professors?"

"I don't think so, but we were under the tarp pretty quickly."

His eyes widened. "Wait, you don't think…"

She nodded. "I do."

He looked at the others, still huddled in discussion. "You have to tell them."

Her heart hammered. "But what if I'm wrong?"

He shook his head. "But what if you're right?"

She sighed then raised a hand. "Umm, excuse me."

Everyone stopped and turned toward her.

"I think I might know who the thief is."

Cy Pulos residence

Athens, Greece

"Professor Antoniou! What are you doing here? Did they find your wife?"

Acton saw Antoniou's ears go red at the young grad student's question. "How do you know about that, Cy?"

"It's all over the news. Is she okay?"

Antoniou shook his head. "No. She's being held because they think I have the urn, and they've beaten her viciously—" His voice cracked as he momentarily lost control. He drew a deep breath. "They've beaten her. I must have the urn, or they're going to kill her."

"But I thought they already had it?"

Antoniou's cheeks joined his ears. "We both know that's not true."

Pulos' eyes narrowed then her cheeks paled. "Wait, do you think I have it?"

Antoniou pushed her apartment door open, barging inside. "Yes. Just tell me where it is, and I won't report you to the police. I just want the urn so that I can give it to them and get Juno back."

"You can't just come in here!"

Acton followed reluctantly, certain they were breaking countless laws, but since Reading was with them, he assumed the Interpol agent would be the one taking the real heat.

"Over here!"

They all followed Laura's voice and soon found her in the kitchen, half a dozen artifacts laid out carefully on the table.

Antoniou's stared at her, wide-eyed. "Cy, what have you done?" He grabbed her by the shoulders, shaking her. "Where is the urn? Tell me!"

Acton and Reading pulled the distraught man off the clearly terrified woman, and she retreated into the corner, fear in her eyes, her arms held up to shield herself from any further assault. "I-I don't have it, Professor. I swear! I was just bringing work home to try and help." She lowered her arms. "I knew you wouldn't want me to, so I didn't tell you. I was just trying to help."

Antoniou stared at her, incredulous. "Help? How is this possibly helping?"

Pulos stared at the floor, as if afraid of the damage her words might cause. "I know about your money problems. We all do. I thought if I did some of the work off-site, then it might help with the budget problems."

Acton stared at the table. The artifacts were being treated with care, and all evidence was that they were being cleaned and cataloged according to procedure.

As any thief might before selling them.

And as any grad student might, if at a dig site.

Antoniou shook his head. "I don't believe you. I want to believe you, but I *can't* believe you."

Reading pulled out his phone. "It's time to get the police involved. I'll call the major."

Pulos burst into tears as Reading made the call, and Laura brought her into the living room, placing her on a couch as Acton and Leather continued to search the apartment. By the time the major and several of his men arrived, they had found nothing beyond what was on the table already, and were instead sitting quietly as no one said anything.

Reading spoke with Major Nicolo for several minutes in the kitchen, then they both entered the living room, Nicolo clearly not pleased. "I should arrest you all."

Acton resisted the urge to point out the fact that seemed to be the man's default position.

"But we'll sort that all out later. Your illegal search could destroy any case we have against the woman."

Antoniou shot to his feet. "I don't give a damn about your case. I want my wife, and she has what I need to get her!"

"The urn."

"Yes, the urn!"

Nicolo turned to the girl. "And you claim you don't have it?"

She shook her head vigorously. "I don't, I swear!"

"We'll sort it out at the station." He motioned to the officers who quickly cuffed the sobbing woman, then led her from the apartment.

Nicolo jabbed a finger at them all. "Go back to your hotel room and stay there. If I catch you interfering again, I *will* arrest you." He turned on Reading. "And *you* should know better!"

Reading's knuckles turned white as his fists clenched, but he remained outwardly calm. "I'd like to sit in on the interrogation."

Nicolo regarded him for a moment, then nodded. "Very well."

They were ushered out of the apartment, and Acton, Laura, Antoniou, and Leather remained silent until they climbed in their SUV.

Laura spoke first. "I don't know about anyone else, but I'm not so sure. Could she be telling the truth?"

Antoniou vehemently shook his head as Leather pulled away from the curb. "She can't be. We know it was stolen, and like your young lady said, she's the only one who could have done it."

Acton pursed his lips, not bothering to correct the distraught man's interpretation of Mai's suggestion. Mai's photo showing Pulos among the cars in the parking lot, rather than in the pit, merely suggested a possibility, not a certainty. "Let's get back to the hotel and see if Tommy has had any luck with tracing those text messages."

The rest of the ride was silent, none wanting to state the obvious.

If Pulos was innocent, then who could have possibly stolen the artifact?

Outside the Antoniou Residence

Athens, Greece

Rafiq spotted the police car first, parked across the street from Professor Antoniou's modest home. He pressed the phone against his ear so he'd have an excuse to be covering his face, and turned away from the window. "Go around to the next street."

Zaman nodded, driving past the police watching the house, then around the corner, without drawing any attention. "What do we do now?"

Rafiq thought for a moment. They needed time. Killing the police then entering the house could lead to near-immediate discovery, and they'd have no time to search for the artifact. Break in from the rear, and there was a chance of being seen by the neighbors, but that was less likely than two dead cops in their car on a public street going unnoticed.

He decided. "Let's try the back. Once we're in, you watch the cops and make sure they stay put while I search."

Zaman nodded and they both climbed out, heading down an alleyway running behind the homes. When they reached the Antoniou's gate, Rafiq tried the handle and it swung open, security at this point evidently not a concern, though the loud screech might as well have been an alarm. They both entered and Rafiq closed the gate as quickly as he could, there no avoiding the squeaky hinges. They both rushed to the rear door and the slight cover its awning offered. Zaman tried the keys taken from the wife's purse as Rafiq scanned the windows of the neighbors, finding no prying eyes.

"Got it!" hissed Zaman as he pushed the door open. Rafiq held him back, listening for the telltale chirp of a security system.

None.

They stepped inside and Rafiq closed the door behind them, again checking for nosy neighbors as Zaman headed to the front of the house and took up position on a couch that gave him a full view of the street with their police chaperones. It didn't take long for Rafiq to search all the obvious places in the small home, coming up empty.

"This is ridiculous," he growled. "Have those cops moved?"

Zaman shook his head. "No, they're still there, drinking coffee."

"I'm putting an end to this, right now." He pulled out his phone and texted the husband.

We're in your house. Tell us where it is or she dies.

King George Hotel
Athens, Greece

The suite was getting a little crowded, which was saying something considering its size. A four-man security team had arrived from Leather's Greek contact, though Korba's men were now heading back into the hallway, their briefing from Leather complete.

Tommy held up the phone. "We've got another message."

Acton leaned forward, placing a hand on Antoniou's shoulder as a show of support. "What does it say?"

"We're in your house. Tell us where it is or she dies."

Laura's hand darted to her mouth. "Should we tell the police? They could arrest them now, since we know where they are."

Leather shook his head. "No, these are the types that are willing to die for their cause. There's no way they have her with them, and they'll happily die in a shootout with the police before they tell us where they're holding her."

Laura nodded. "Of course. Then what do we do? We have to respond."

Acton took the phone from Tommy. "We have to tell them it was never there."

Antoniou looked at him with tear-filled eyes. "And if they ask where it is?"

"We have to be vague." Acton waved the cellphone. "That's one advantage of this type of communication. It gives us time to think." He smiled. "How about this?" He quickly typed a message then read it aloud. "It was never there. Be careful, I think the police are watching my house." He smiled. "I'm thinking a show of concern for their safety might throw them off a bit, make our story a little more believable."

Laura nodded. "I like it."

Acton held up the phone. "Everyone agree?"

Bobbing heads circled the room and he pressed send.

"Done. Now we have to figure out what our next response is. They're going to want to know where it is, and we can't keep avoiding the question."

Tommy slapped his hands together, glee on his face. "Found them!"

Laura gave him a look. "Let me guess, Professor Antoniou's house?"

Tommy laughed. "Nooo, I mean I know where he was when he was sending the original text messages." He spun the laptop, several pulsing red dots displayed on a map of Athens. Antoniou pointed at one of them.

"That's my home."

"Yes, that's where they are now. But these"—Tommy pointed at a small cluster of dots—"are where they were when they sent the original messages."

Acton peered at the map. "That looks like it's about ten minutes from here."

Leather nodded. "That makes sense. They want to do an exchange, and they'll want to do it quickly, so they won't want to waste time traveling."

Laura let out an exasperated sigh. "So, what do we do?"

Acton pointed at the screen. "We need eyes on that place."

Leather shook his head. "We can't risk going there. If they're watching the hotel, they could follow us and know we found them. They might kill her."

Acton frowned. "We have to tell the police. I don't see that we have any other choice."

Antoniou shook his head vehemently. "Absolutely not. They could raid the place and get her killed."

Acton looked at him. "Then what should we do?"

Tommy raised a finger. "Umm, I have an idea."

Outside the Suqut Brigade Safe House
Athens, Greece

Tankov listened to the report from his man assigned to follow the vehicle that had left earlier. He had tracked it to the professor's house, and the Suqut Brigade members had just left, empty-handed.

He turned to Utkin. "It's not at the professor's house, and it wasn't at the grad student's apartment." He shook his head. "I get the distinct impression that nobody who should know where it is, does know where it is. This is ridiculous."

Utkin agreed. "There must be a third team."

Tankov shook his head. "No, if there were, then Damos would have known, and after what they did to him, there's no way he didn't talk."

"Then it has to be an inside job. That's the only other explanation."

Tankov pursed his lips. "Then who? It's not at the professor's house, and we're dealing with her life. Surely if they had it, they would have handed it over by now. Nobody's that greedy."

Utkin shrugged. "I am."

"Yes, but you're a little touched. These are professors."

"They're always the crazy ones in the movies."

Tankov chuckled. "True." He tapped his chin. "Okay, why did they go to the grad student's apartment? They obviously thought she had it."

"And she was taken away in handcuffs, so obviously the police think she has it too."

"Then why not just hand it over?"

"Maybe the authorities won't let them?"

Tankov smiled. "Or they still don't know where it is. Vasiliev said that they left empty-handed. Nothing big enough that could have held the artifact."

"So, she's not cooperating, because she *is* greedy enough to let the wife die." Utkin sighed dreamily. "Sounds like my kind of woman."

"Okay, if we assume she stole it, then where is it?" He snapped his fingers then pointed at the keyboard. "Run her name and see if she owns or rents any other property. Maybe she's hidden it somewhere other than her apartment."

King George Hotel

Athens, Greece

"Is this legal?"

Tommy didn't look at Acton to answer his question, his attention instead focused exactly where it should be, on the large screen in front of them. He had somehow jacked into the hotel room's television so everyone could see what was happening, rather than having them crowd around his laptop.

And the extra effort spent while waiting for the equipment to be readied by Korba's team was worth it.

"Legal? Definitely not, but they'd have to catch me first, and I never get caught."

Acton eyed him. "Oh, *really?*"

Tommy risked a quick glance. "Okay, once." He grinned. "But I'm much better now."

"Uh huh." Acton jabbed a finger at the screen and Tommy returned his attention to it, leaning to his left as he adjusted the trajectory of the drone he was controlling with his laptop. Korba's team had been able to supply the equipment needed to implement Tommy's idea, and the drone had been launched from one of their vehicles, saving them precious minutes.

Antoniou pointed at the screen. "I think we're getting close."

Tommy nodded, swiftly bringing the drone to a halt and panning the camera down, showing half a dozen rooftops. "We're here." He centered a target over the rooftop in the middle of the screen, directly below the drone. "This is it. Let me see what we're dealing with." A flurry of keystrokes had them all in suspense as they waited for the computer genius to give them something, anything, that they could work with.

He smiled.

"I've got a bunch of wi-fi signals and cellular signals of course, but a few are pretty strong that could be coming from the building. I'm going to see if I can tap into them."

More keystrokes were followed by a "Huh."

Acton's eyes narrowed. "What?"

"Well, a few of these signals look like they might be video feeds."

Laura leaned forward. "Security cameras?"

"Could be. If I can tap them, we might be able to…" His voice drifted as he worked his magic. "I'm in." He looked up at the television screen as it flickered, the live feed from the drone's camera replaced by the image of a badly beaten man.

Laura gasped. "Oh my! Is he alive?"

Acton rose, stepping closer to the screen, then pointed. "His chest is moving. He's breathing." He cursed. "They did quite the number on him."

"I've got another one." The screen flickered again, and the feed of the man was replaced by a black screen.

"What's wrong?" asked Acton as he returned to his chair.

Tommy shrugged. "Weird. The signal seems good, so we should be seeing something."

Mai pointed at the screen. "I can see something. Shadows maybe? Perhaps it's closed curtains?"

Acton thought it was as good a suggestion as any. "Could be. Any other feeds?"

"One more." The screen flickered again and Antoniou leaped to his feet. "Juno!"

Acton cringed as the woman sat with her back to them, her head turned to the side giving them an angle that revealed a bloody nose and swollen lip, along with a black eye that Acton feared had a match on the other side of her face.

She's been punched in the nose.

Acton chose to look at the positive, grabbing Antoniou's shoulder and giving him a shake. "She's alive. This is good news."

Antoniou wiped the tears from his cheeks, nodding. "Yes, I suppose it is. It's just…"

"I know, my friend, I know." And he did. He had seen the aftermath of his wife being beaten, and it was heartbreaking, and rage inducing. And right now, he knew Antoniou was feeling helpless and useless.

Tommy pointed to the left side of the frame. "Someone's coming."

A man with a thick beard entered the room, standing in front of her, and Juno struggled against her bonds, the man saying something to her, anger on his face.

"Is there audio?" asked Laura.

"Just a sec." Tommy hit a few keys and suddenly they heard voices behind a heavy hiss of white noise. "I'll try to clean it up." A few more keystrokes and the hiss dropped dramatically as the man removed what appeared to be a gag from Juno's mouth.

"I need to use the bathroom."

"Not my problem."

"You want me to pee right here?"

"I don't care."

"It will stink. Do you really want that?"

The man stared at her for a moment then growled, reaching forward and cutting the ties binding her arms to the chair. He yanked her to her feet then marched her toward the door.

"Try anything, and you die."

They both disappeared from the frame and Antoniou sighed, reaching for the image of his wife. "She's alive," he whispered.

Acton nodded. "Yes. And we know where she is. I think we have to tell the police."

"We can't. She could die."

Acton shook his head. "I'm sorry, Basil, but we don't have the urn, and we have no idea where it is. Eventually, these guys will get tired of our delays and kill her anyway."

Antoniou sighed. "You're right. We don't have a choice."

Acton grabbed his phone. "I'll bring Hugh up to date and let him deal with the major."

Outside the Suqut Brigade Safe House
Athens, Greece

Tankov stared with interest at the three monitors showing the inside of the house their targets occupied, this the first time the woman had been moved since they had activated the surveillance equipment. He focused on the camera showing Damos, as the other two had nothing of interest.

"Look." He pointed at the screen showing Damos staring at the door, his jaw dropping and his eyes widening. He struggled against his bonds for a moment, but quickly gave up, the beating he had evidently received sapping him of his strength. Tankov leaned back in the too small chair, one of four in the large van that housed their security operation. "Which way is the bathroom?"

Utkin pointed at the rear door. "Out there, pick a bush."

"That's not what I meant."

Utkin tapped the screen in front of him. "I've finished the search. Do you want to hear about our grad student?"

Tankov spun in his chair. "Give it to me."

"She doesn't have any other property, rented or otherwise, under her name."

Tankov frowned. "Parents?"

"They live in Katerini. Northern Greece. She wouldn't have had time to get there and back."

"Sure she would."

Utkin shook his head. "No, remember, they were all at the police station for over five hours last night. If she stole it when these guys attacked, she couldn't have taken it with her, and they've got that entire area cordoned off, with police everywhere." He jabbed a finger at her file. "I think she stole it, hid it somewhere on-site, and is waiting for an opportunity to go back once things cool down."

Tankov's head slowly bobbed. "That makes sense. The Brigade attacks, she takes advantage of the situation, probably knowing all along when it was going to happen, so she's prepared. She hides it somewhere nobody is going to think to look, the police arrive, take them all in for questioning, and seal off the place. If they find it, they still don't know she's the one behind it, and if they don't, she just waits for the right time to retrieve it." He smiled. "Clever girl."

Utkin. "Dibs."

"Careful. This one sounds cold."

Utkin grinned. "My kind of woman."

"Every woman is your kind of woman."

Utkin's head bobbed. "This is true. I am a man of *un*discriminating taste."

"I think you're a man who is determined to try every item at the buffet at least once."

Utkin eyed him. "And what's wrong with that?"

Tankov laughed. "I can't think of a single thing at the moment." His eyes narrowed and he pointed at the screen. "She has a car registered under her name." His heart skipped a beat. "If she drives to work, maybe she stashed the urn inside."

Utkin pursed his lips, staring at the screen. "Definitely possible."

A smile spread on Tankov's face. "And with the police sealing it off, it's probably still there." He jabbed a finger at the display. "We have to get inside that car."

Hellenic Police Headquarters
Athens, Greece

"We know you stole the urn. Why deny it?"

Reading stood in the corner, looking intimidating, as Major Nicolo continued the interrogation of the young grad student, Cy Pulos. For his benefit, Nicolo was conducting it in English, which he felt might trip the woman up, since she'd have to think harder than if she were speaking in her native tongue. He had to admit it was a good idea, and had the added benefit of letting him understand the proceedings, rather than listening to incoherent babble.

Though nothing had been revealed as of yet. The woman had so far stuck to her story, and had also unwisely refused a lawyer, indicating she feared it might make her appear guilty.

Always demand a lawyer.

"I swear to you, I never took it. I have no idea where it is!"

Nicolo tossed several photos onto the table showing the artifacts found in her apartment. "You expect me to believe that, when you stole these?"

Tears flowed down her face once again. "Like I've told you so many times before, I take my work home with me. I always return it the next day. You've searched my apartment. You know I don't have it."

"You could have hidden it somewhere else."

"When would I have had the time? They attacked the site, then you guys showed up, and we were all taken here. I swear to you I wasn't stealing those artifacts. I was just processing them and cataloging them to save time and money. Each day, I bring them back and give them to one of the professors."

Nicolo paused, picking up on something she said. "If this is true, you giving them to the professor, then why was he so surprised that you had them?"

"Because I never told him I did the work at home! He just assumed I was efficient, I guess."

"Why not just tell him what you were doing?"

"Because it was against protocol. He wouldn't have approved."

"Yet you still did it."

She sighed, her voice dropping to a near whisper. "Only to help him. He's such a sweet man, and I knew money was desperately tight. They are always threatening to shut us down, and if it weren't for our anonymous donors, we would have been shut down months ago."

Nicolo's eyes narrowed. "Anonymous donors? Who?"

She eyeballed him. "Umm, *anonymous* donors. What part of that don't you understand?"

Nicolo leaned in, knuckles on the table. "Don't get smart with me, young lady."

She recoiled in her seat, her head dropping, eyes on her hands folded in her lap. "Sorry. I-I don't know who they are. Donations would come in through a website one of the guys set up for Professor Galanos. I don't know any more than that."

"Who set it up?"

"Ezio. Ask him about it, maybe he can tell you more."

Nicolo checked his notepad. "Ezio Remes. We had him in here last night."

"Yes, he was at the dig site when those men attacked."

Nicolo paced the room for a moment, saying nothing, then whirled on Pulos. "You want to know what I think?"

She trembled. "No?"

Reading suppressed a smile.

"I think *you* are the anonymous donor. You steal small items, you clean them up, you sell them, then you donate the money back."

Her eyes widened with horror. "Why would I do that?"

"You said it yourself. You think the professor is a sweet man. You empathize with his situation. If you run out of money, then the dig is shut down, affecting your livelihood. By helping fund it through stolen goods, you get to keep your job. Keep paying your bills."

She stared at him, wide-eyed. "But I'd be stealing history! Nobody has that right!"

She sounds like Jim and Laura.

"Somebody there thought they did, and you're all archaeologists, aren't you? There have been thefts from your site for months."

She frowned, her shoulders slumping. "I know. It's terrible."

"Do you know who's behind it?"

She shook her head. "No idea, except that it's not me."

"You, an intelligent young woman doesn't even have a theory? I find that hard to believe."

She regarded him for a moment, then looked away. "I had always assumed it was one of the guards. They're the only ones with access to the site after everyone goes home." She looked up at him. "Can I go now? I have to feed my cat."

Nicolo chuckled, shaking his head. "You're not going anywhere. You're being charged with theft."

Her face paled. "But I'm innocent!"

"That will be for a court to decide."

She leaned forward. "Please, you can't do this to me. I'll lose my job, and I'll be kicked out of the program. I have bills to pay. I just bought a new car! Please, let me talk to Professor Antoniou. Let me explain everything to him. I'm sure once he calms down he'll realize I was only trying to help."

Reading stepped forward. "New car?"

Nicolo stared at him for a moment, not happy that their agreement for him to stand there quietly had been broken. "That's right, a new car. How could you afford that on a graduate student's salary?"

She scoffed at him. "It's not some fancy British sports car!"

Reading grunted. "You couldn't afford the repair bills on one of those."

Nicolo grinned. "Or the second car you'd need while it's in the shop."

Reading stared at her, wiping the smile from his face. "Just where is this car now?"

Outside the Suqut Brigade Safe House

Athens, Greece

Tankov watched the video streamed to them by his men now at the dig site. And cursed. There was still a police presence, though not heavy. Enough, however, to prevent them from casually strolling in.

"What do you want us to do?"

Tankov stared at the camera feeds of the house they had been sitting on. There appeared to be nothing going on here for the moment, but if they were to leave, they'd lose the signal.

"Sir?"

A decision had to be made. "Okay, I'm on the way. Pull the detail off the hotel and have them join me." He rose, slapping Utkin on the back. "And put trackers on their vehicles, just in case they all leave and split up."

Utkin nodded. "Consider it done." He eyeballed him. "Are you going to kill cops?"

Tankov frowned, thinking of his new philosophy, then sighed. "Let's hope it doesn't become necessary."

"And if it does?"

Tankov shrugged. "Nobody's perfect."

King George Hotel

Athens, Greece

"We're almost at the dig. We think it might be in her car that she left there."

Acton glanced at Antoniou, hope on all their faces at the news from Reading. Then Antoniou appeared worried, and Acton knew why. He leaned toward the phone sitting on the table, its speaker active "But, Hugh, if the police find it, we'll never be able to use it to exchange for Juno."

"I know, but things are out of my control at this point. This is a Greek police matter, and Interpol is only observing and providing advice. At least if we know where it is, that's one piece of the puzzle solved."

Acton nodded. "And I guess it will confirm that Cy was behind the thefts, so two pieces solved."

"Right. Unfortunately, neither of those help us find Professor Antoniou's wife."

Acton glanced at the others, and Laura shrugged. "You have to tell him."

"Tell me what?"

Acton rolled his eyes at his wife. "Sure, throw me under the bus." He leaned toward the phone. "We, well, we sort of found her."

"What? Why didn't you tell me?"

"We didn't want you to have to lie to the Greeks."

There was a pause. "Wait, are you saying she isn't with you?"

"No, she isn't. We found where they're holding her."

"How?"

Acton glanced at Tommy. "Do you really want to know?"

There was a grunt. "No, but give Tommy a smack to the back of the head for me."

Tommy grinned and Mai beamed with pride.

Acton regarded Antoniou for a moment, the man's breathing becoming more rapid as reality set in. "Well, once you have the urn, we'll have nothing to leverage for Juno anymore. I don't think we have any choice but to come clean so the police can deal with the situation." He put a hand on Antoniou's shoulder. "Basil, do you agree?"

He sighed, then nodded. "Reluctantly."

A burst of static and a grunt from the phone suggested Reading was on the move. "We just arrived. Let's see what's in this car. This entire conversation could be moot if it's not there. I'll call you back in a few minutes."

Phaleron Delta Necropolis

Athens, Greece

Tankov watched through binoculars as a car pulled through the gate of the dig site, two men exiting. A slight smile crept up his face as he recognized one of them.

"Does this change anything?"

He glanced at the driver, Vasiliev, and shook his head. "I know one of them. He'll be unarmed. Let's proceed."

Vasiliev started the SUV's engine and pulled out onto the road, merging into the light evening traffic, then put his signal light on, casually turning onto the unpaved road leading to the gate.

"Quick and clean, people," whispered Tankov, a smile on his face as all four windows rolled down to greet the private security and police that approached.

Vasiliev leaned out the window. "We were hoping for a tour. Any chance?"

One of the officers appeared annoyed and jabbed a finger at the road behind them. "No tours. Back it up and move along."

Vasiliev nodded. "Sorry to hear that."

"Now." Tankov raised his Remington 870 Tac-14 shotgun and fired a single Taser eXtended Range Electro-Muscular Projectile into each of the two guards in his arc, the others taking out their targets equally as efficiently with the XREP rounds. Somebody shouted from the other side of the gate and Vasiliev hammered on the gas, blasting through it as they raced toward the grad student's car, its location identified by the advance team.

And where the two new arrivals had parked.

Tankov fired another round at what appeared to be private security and frowned as the non-lethal shell they had been using embedded itself uselessly in the man's vest.

He cursed. "Okay, switch to lethal."

Reading dove for cover as gunfire tore across the parking lot. At least half a dozen were down at the main gate, and whoever was in the SUV appeared extremely well trained, their shots far too efficiently taking out what security remained.

Heavy gunfire erupted from one of Leather's Greek team, taking out the engine block, a burst of steam hissing from under the hood, bringing the attackers to a halt, though not halting the attack. Four doors opened and an equal number of hostiles emerged as Reading repositioned near one of the Greek team.

"Weapon!"

The man tossed him a Glock without looking, then two magazines. "Make'em count."

Reading sprinted as fast as his old bones could carry him to try and set up a crossfire when someone cried out behind him. He dropped to the ground, rolling behind a vehicle, then cursed as he spotted the man who had armed him, lying on the ground, out of commission and perhaps dead.

Nicolo slammed into the car beside him, his weapon at the ready. "What are we going to do?"

Reading shook his head, scanning the area before popping up and firing several rounds ineffectually. "I suspect we're going to die."

"Not today, Agent Reading."

They both spun to find one of the attackers standing behind them, a gun in each hand, trained on them both. Reading cursed, tossing his onto the ground, Nicolo doing the same.

Reading stared up at the man. "Do I know you?"

The man shook his head as the gunfire dwindled to nothing, the battle lost. "No, but I know you." He flicked his weapon. "Get up."

They both rose, Reading with a little more of a struggle than he cared to have had witnessed by others. He brushed off his clothes, then stared at the man. "How do you know me?"

"I know your friends. Two annoying archaeology professors."

Reading frowned. "And how do you know them?"

The man shook his head. "Unimportant." He motioned toward Pulos' car. "I see you figured it out."

Reading nodded. "As did you."

The man ushered them over to the car, the others joining them, taking up covering positions, then raised his weapon to shoot out the trunk's lock.

Nicolo cleared his throat, holding up a key. "Perhaps I can be of assistance?"

The man chuckled, stepping back. "Please."

Nicolo unlocked the trunk, the lid popping up automatically. They all leaned in, then smiled at the sight.

A large item, wrapped in a blanket.

The man flicked his wrist. "Agent Reading, would you do the honors?"

Reading stepped forward and carefully unwrapped whatever the blanket was protecting, but with each turn, any doubts he might have had as to what it was, faded.

As well as any doubt as to who the thief was.

She lied to us the entire time.

With a final pull on the blanket, the urn was revealed, and Reading, as was so often the case, was underwhelmed.

Just another clay jar.

He stepped back. "Is this what you were looking for?"

The man nodded, then snapped his fingers, two of his men rushing forward with a large case. The urn was packaged carefully, probably to standards Acton would have been pleased with.

Reading turned to the man. "Now that you have what you came for, will you release Professor Galanos?"

The man regarded him for a moment, then shook his head. "Agent Reading, we never had her." He raised his shotgun and fired, hitting Reading square in the chest.

Phaleron Delta Necropolis
Athens, Greece

Reading groaned, his entire body aching as he tried to make sense of what had just happened. Finally able to open his eyes and relax his muscles, he suddenly grabbed at his chest, searching for a wound he knew wasn't there—if it were, he'd be dead, or in a hell of a lot more pain than he was.

Instead, it felt like he had just run a marathon.

What's this?

He pulled a strange device from his chest then said a silent prayer of thanks as he was reminded of dealing with the Triarii and their non-lethal modus operandi. Though why these men had employed similar methods, he wasn't sure. He rolled to his feet and surveyed the area. The hostiles were gone, and several of the guards were on their feet, checking on the others. Nicolo stood nearby, on his phone. He waved at Reading, continuing his conversation.

234

Reading pulled out his phone, just then realizing that the grad student's car was gone, the SUV the hostiles had arrived in sitting nearby, out of commission with a bullet-riddled engine block. He called Acton.

"Hugh, what's going on? I've been calling you."

"We were attacked."

"What? Are you okay?"

"I am, but I think some of the guards might be dead. Some are definitely wounded. They used some weird Taser-like thing on most of us. I've never seen anything like it. They didn't work on Korba's men because they had body armor, so they took the brunt of it."

Acton cursed. "I, umm, hate to sound self-centered, but did you find the urn?"

"We did. It was in her trunk, exactly as we suspected."

"That's great! At least we finally have some answers. Where is it now?"

"The guys who attacked us took it."

There was a pause. "Then I guess that's good news as well, right? Now that they have it, they'll let Juno go."

Reading shook his head. "The guy doing all the talking said they never had her. I think this is a different group. They were well-equipped, dressed as special ops types, and the guy who spoke didn't look Arab at all. Definitely Caucasian."

"Did you get them on camera?"

"I'm not sure. I literally just woke up. But right now, I don't think our Suqut Brigade guys know the urn has been found."

Acton sighed. "But once they find out, Juno is no longer of any use to them. I think we have to hit them now, before the press finds out."

Reading agreed. "I'll give the address you sent me to Nicolo."

"Okay, just tell them to be careful. We don't want a repeat of Portugal."

"No, we don't." Reading paused as he remembered the rest of the conversation he had with the hostile. "Jim, there's something else."

"What?"

"The man who led the attack here…"

"Yes?"

"He says he knows you and Laura."

King George Hotel

Athens, Greece

Adelaide sat curled up on a chaise lounge near the window, a laptop perched beside her, as she reviewed all the video captured from the house holding the professor's wife.

Just like at work.

This was what she did. She sat in a dark room inside the embassy, monitoring security footage, watching for anything out of the ordinary from the visitors inside the grounds, and those loitering on the outside.

And she was trained to follow people from camera to camera, observing their interactions with others who weren't in the previous camera's frame.

She smiled, replaying what she had caught to be sure. She turned to the room, deep in discussion over what had just been said by Agent Reading—that this second team knew the Actons. It was an interesting development, one that made no sense to her, but from what she was discovering in dribs and drabs, the people in this room were wealthy, well connected, and always in trouble.

She stared at Leather, still manning the door, and felt a twinge in her core. This was a man. A *real* man. Not some coddled millennial raised by helicopter parents. This was a man who had served his country, had fought God only knew how many evil people, and now protected the people inside this room, along with the students they were responsible for.

This was a man she could see herself with.

Though it was too soon to be planning a wedding.

She cleared her throat. "Sorry to interrupt, but I found something you're going to want to see." She held up her laptop and Tommy walked over with his. He synced up the feeds then played them on the hotel room's large screen. "Can you do a split screen? The man's room on the left, the professor's on the right?"

Tommy shrugged. "Sure." The screen split.

"Okay, play them both at the same time."

Tommy tapped a key and both images began playing. "Now, on the right we see Juno being taken to the bathroom. They head out the door and to the left, then we lose sight of them. A few seconds later, we see the man our hostage-takers have referred to as 'the fence,' stare at the door, his jaw drops, and his eyes widen, and he struggles for a few moments, as if agitated about something."

"You think he saw Juno?" asked Acton.

"Yes."

"But how can we be sure?"

"Tommy, replay it, but let's pay attention to the top left of the screen. Watch the floor."

The image replayed, and Adelaide pointed at the part of the image she wanted everyone to focus on, a brighter spot that was the reflection of a light coming from somewhere outside the room. Two shadows momentarily blocked the light, just before the man reacted.

"Did you see it?"

Laura nodded. "Two people went by, one after the other."

"Exactly, and then he reacted. It has to be Juno and the hostage-taker walking by. It would be too much of a coincidence for another two people to be going by at the same time."

Acton agreed. "Okay, but what does it mean? Is he reacting to Juno specifically, to the fact there's a woman who has been badly beaten, or simply to the fact there's another hostage in the house with him?"

Adelaide shrugged. "It could be any or none."

Tommy chuckled. "Maybe he wanted to go to the bathroom too."

Mai swatted him.

Acton smiled. "Unfortunately, it could be as simple as that. But let's think this through. I don't think he'd care if someone else was there, surely not enough to draw any more attention to himself after the torture he's clearly undergone."

Laura pursed her lips. "I think he's reacting to Juno herself. I think he recognized her."

Antoniou shook his head. "Why would my wife know a man like that?"

Acton leaned back and folded his arms. "Maybe he knows her, but she doesn't know him?"

Antoniou shrugged. "It's possible, I guess. She's the one I put out in front of the press whenever there's a discovery. I'm too camera shy." His eyes widened. "And she used to be an Olympian! A decathlete! She was quite popular here in Greece when she was younger. Perhaps he recognized her from back then."

Acton's head bobbed. "Possible." He sighed. "Or maybe we're just reading too much into this."

"What do you mean?"

"I mean, if I were a hostage, and saw a woman who had been beaten, I'd get pretty pissed too." He pointed at the screen. "Just show us his footage. Replay his reaction. Can you zoom in?"

Tommy nodded, and the image changed to a single feed, zoomed in on the man's face. "Good thing this is HD."

The image played, the man's jaw dropping then his eyes widening before narrowing, followed by gyrations as he struggled for a few moments against his bonds.

Acton rose, approaching the screen. "Okay, replay it again, now watch his eyes." The image played and Acton pointed. "See, his eyes widen, then they narrow, then he struggles, with them narrowed. Now, what emotions does that suggest to you?"

Adelaide smiled, the professor astute even outside of a dig site. "Surprise then anger."

Acton snapped his fingers then returned to his seat. "Exactly. He sees her, his eyes widen in surprise, then they narrow in anger. The question is why. If he recognized her, then we have to assume the anger is because they've hurt someone he knows. If he doesn't, then he's angry because of how they treated a woman."

Laura frowned. "A chivalrous criminal?"

Acton shrugged. "They do exist."

Antoniou grunted. "To be frank, I couldn't care less about him. He can die for all I care. I only care about my wife. And I fear the police will end up killing her in their zeal for revenge over what just happened at the dig site."

Acton frowned. "We've seen it before. Maybe we should go there?"

Leather strode quickly into the center of the conversation, sending Adelaide's heart pumping. "Absolutely not. Bullets could be flying, or worse." He turned to Antoniou, calming his tone. "I'm sorry, Professor, but the best thing for your wife is for us to be out from underfoot. We'll monitor this footage, and make sure they don't move her. If they do, we'll be able to tell them." He turned to Tommy. "Can you send this feed to the police?"

"Sure. I just need to know where."

"I'll find out for you." Leather disappeared into the bedroom and Adelaide sighed.

"Isn't he amazing?"

Acton grinned. "Yup. If I weren't straight, I'd be all over him."

Tommy and Mai snickered.

Adelaide smiled at Acton. "He warned me about you two. Always getting into trouble."

"True, but it's almost never our fault."

"Almost?"

Acton shrugged. "Sometimes it is. Nobody's perfect."

Leather returned, a frown on his face. He handed his phone to Tommy. "Everything you need should be there."

Tommy quickly read what was on the display and nodded, going to work.

Leather pulled a knife from his belt then slapped it on Acton's chest, the blade flat. "See, he's a damned magnet for trouble. I should have stayed in the Regiment. It would have been safer, but nooo, I had to retire to the good life."

Laura grinned as Leather sheathed his knife. "So, you admit it's a good life?"

Adelaide laughed. "She's got you there!"

Leather looked at her. "See, I can't win with these two."

She smiled. "But you do seem happy."

"I know! So what does that make me?"

Acton grunted. "Some sort of fool, I'm sure. There's probably a clinical term for it, but I'm an archaeologist, not a psychologist."

Leather growled. "I should be committed for sticking around you two."

Acton gave two exaggerated thumbs up. "I know someone! Consider it done!"

Outside the Suqut Brigade Safe House

Athens, Greece

"Time for Phase Two."

Utkin grinned. "I love Phase Twos. Phase Ones are always boring."

Tankov chuckled. "I'd hardly call taking out over a dozen police and private security boring."

"True, but most of them were taken out with non-lethals. Phase Two is totally lethal."

Tankov had to agree. This was what they were trained for. Recovery of the item had proven fun, and he did regret possibly killing some of the guards since they were just doing their job, but it was kill or be killed, and when forced to choose, it was always kill. Turning over a new leaf was proving more difficult than he had thought, though a few months ago, everyone at the dig site would now be dead, instead of just a few. And in all honesty, he wasn't even sure if they had killed anyone, though they had certainly severely wounded a few.

But now that the artifact had been recovered—Phase One—it was time to fulfill the second part of their mission as assigned by Sheik Khalid.

Elimination of the Suqut Brigade members that had betrayed him.

The fact they hadn't, was of no concern to Tankov. These were Islamic extremists, and though innocent of crossing Khalid, they were still guilty of trying to take over the world in a violent jihad.

They deserved to die.

And so they would.

Besides, he had already been paid a deposit to do so, and he had plans for that money.

What the sheik doesn't know can't hurt him.

Vasiliev, his face on a monitor to Tankov's left, chimed in. "I think there might only be four of them left. Not so much fun."

Utkin agreed. "Thanks to the Greeks, they're down a half-dozen, but it'll still be satisfying to rid the planet of the rest of them. Should we hit them here and get it over with?"

Tankov chewed his cheek for a moment, staring at the monitors. "I don't know. It's really tight quarters, and we don't know the layout. The rear entrance is boarded up, so there's only the front. They could have it rigged to explode." He shook his head. "No, I think we need to force them out, then take them on our own terms."

Utkin shrugged. "We could always make a second entrance. Blow out the rear wall then just walk in shooting."

"No. These houses are packed so tightly together that any explosion like that could take out the neighbors and kill innocent people. This isn't Chechnya where we don't care. This is Europe. And if we did that, we'd also be guaranteeing that Professor Antoniou's wife would be killed."

"Not to mention that Damos guy."

Tankov grunted. "I don't give a shit about him, he's a criminal."

Utkin raised a finger. "Like us."

Tankov smiled. "We're high-class."

Utkin struck a pose. "And more handsome."

Tankov laughed. "Well, I won't comment on that. Bottom line is that this will be more difficult than it would have been in the old days, but when have we ever run away from a challenge?"

Utkin grinned. "Not since Vasiliev surrendered when you challenged him to a no lap dance rule in Prague."

Vasiliev burst out laughing. "Yeah, I totally failed that one! How long did I last? Six minutes?"

Utkin shrugged. "Only if you're counting the time she was in your lap. You were out so fast, we should be calling you Cosmo Kramer."

Tankov joined the laughter then turned serious. "Okay, enough of that. We need to get them out of there, and I think I have an idea as to how."

Suqut Brigade Safe House
Athens, Greece

"How long do we wait?"

Zaman's question was a good one, and Rafiq's only answer was that they had already waited too long. Yet what choice did they have? They needed that artifact. If they didn't get it, Sheik Khalid would put a hit out on them, and dying for Allah was one thing, but being assassinated because one failed at stealing something, was another. One guaranteed access to Jannah, the other was doubtful.

Though stealing from the infidel perhaps might be considered honorable. After all, the Koran said it was a sin to lie or cheat, but only a fellow Muslim.

Allah and His Messenger are free from liability to the idolaters.

He knew his Koran, and it guided him through this life so that the next would be eternal bliss.

He just wasn't that interested in getting there so soon unless on the battlefield.

All in good time.

He stared down the hallway, toward where Damos and the woman were held, trying to decide what to do. Every minute they remained here was another minute they could be discovered. Though no one knew about this location, messages had been sent from here, and if the professor went to the police, they could be traced.

But he wouldn't dare.

Would he?

The phone rang and he grabbed it. "Hello?"

"There's a problem."

He tensed at the voice of the lookout he had assigned to the dig site. "What?"

"The site was hit by another team about twenty minutes ago."

"Twenty? What took you so long to report?"

"I figured I better get another burner, just in case they decided to track the phones in the area."

Rafiq grunted. "Good thinking." His eyes narrowed as he sank back in his chair. "Who did they hit?"

"No idea, but they were well armed and well trained. They cut through the guards in minutes."

Rafiq suppressed a curse. "Then?"

"Then they opened the back of a car, removed something, shot a couple more police, then took the car and the item."

"Was it the urn?"

"Looked like it from here."

"Whose car was it?"

"No idea, but I got the plates."

Rafiq exhaled loudly. "Run them. I want to know whose it was. And if that car doesn't belong to the professor, his wife is dead."

"It'll take me a few minutes, but the bottom line is, whoever these guys were, they've got the artifact, and there's no way they work for the professor."

Rafiq shook his head, closing his eyes. "Agreed. Call me as soon as you find out who the owner is."

He ended the call, tugging at his beard in frustration.

"What did he say?"

He opened his eyes and looked at Zaman and the others. "Another team recovered the item."

Zaman cursed. "Then we're dead." He gestured down the hall. "I say we kill them now, get out of here, and figure out how to make the sheik happy without getting ourselves killed."

Rafiq nodded. "I don't think we have a choice anymore. Even if the professor was telling us the truth, and that was his car that had the artifact in it, the fact still remains that he no longer has it. These other guys, and I have a pretty good idea who they are, have it, and my guess is it will be delivered into the hands of the sheik before morning prayers."

An odd sound had him pausing, and he rose, staring about the room. "Do you hear that?"

Zaman shrugged. "I've barely heard anything since Mosul. What?"

"A high-pitched squealing sound." It continued to get louder, and Rafiq stared at the window, certain it was coming from that direction.

Zaman rose. "I can hear it."

They were all on their feet now, searching for the source as it continued to get louder. Rafiq tore open the curtains and stared out the window, but saw nothing.

Zaman pointed at the upper corner. "What's that?"

Rafiq's heart hammered hard and he opened the opposite window, reaching out and yanking the small device from the glass.

"What is it? A detonator?"

Rafiq shook his head as he held it up so the others could see. "It looks like it has a camera and microphone on it."

"Police?"

He shook his head. "No, they would have either hit us by now, or asked us what our demands were." He growled. "This has to belong to the other team. They've been listening in on us the entire time."

Zaman's eyes widened. "But how? How could they possibly know we were here?"

Rafiq stared down the hall. "They must have followed us from Damos' place. That's the only explanation."

Zaman's eyes widened further. "That means they've heard everything for hours!"

Rafiq held the device up to his face, pointing the camera at himself. "I don't know who you are, but you have what I want. I suggest we meet to discuss it." He entered his number on the keypad of his phone, then held it up to the camera. "I'll expect your call."

Outside the Suqut Brigade Safe House
Athens, Greece

Utkin laughed. "Well, that got their attention."

Tankov entered the number displayed on the screen into his phone, smiling broadly. "I had a feeling having the window pane amplify the feedback might."

Utkin pointed at the screen. "Did you see his face? It must have sounded like a phaser on overload in there."

Tankov nodded. "Too bad they probably have no idea what that is." The signal died, those inside evidently deciding they had been spied upon enough. Yet it didn't matter. The entire point of this exercise was to get them out of the house regardless, making the cameras useless to them within the next few minutes.

"What now?"

"Now I think we do as they ask."

"And when they ask for the artifact?"

"I put the fear of their Allah in them."

Utkin grinned then pointed at the camera showing Damos' room. "Something's happening."

King George Hotel

Athens, Greece

"Did you get that number?"

Tommy nodded as everyone gathered around the television, watching the replay of what had just appeared, the third camera, dark until this time, finally showing video. "It matches the one that was sending the text messages to the professor."

Acton smiled. "And now we've got a face to go with it. Send that to Hugh so he can run it."

"Yes, sir."

The new image abruptly went blank.

"What happened?"

Tommy shrugged. "They probably killed it. I would."

Laura pointed at the screen showing three images, one now blank. "Wait, what are they doing now?"

Tommy zoomed in on the feed of the man's room and they all watched as the hostage-taker who had appeared on the camera a few moments ago entered.

"Your time is up."

The man screamed against his gag, his eyes bulging with fear. He rubbed his mouth against his shoulder and the gag tore loose. "No, please wait! I have something important I have to tell you."

The bearded man pointed his weapon at the man's chest. "Sorry, no time."

"But I know who—"

Two shots were fired in rapid succession, cutting off whatever was about to be said, leaving the entire room witnessing the murder in shocked horror.

Adelaide broke the silence. "What do you think he was about to say?"

Acton shook his head. "We'll never know." He snapped his fingers. "Put up Juno's room."

Tommy complied and they all took a collective breath as the shooter entered her room. The gag was yanked loose and her ties were cut.

"Please don't kill me!"

The man shook his head. "We still need you." He fished a phone from his pocket, the flashing display indicating a call. He smiled, holding it up for Juno to see. "But after this call? Who knows?"

Antoniou cried out in despair, looking at the others. "Where are the police?"

En route to the Suqut Brigade Safe House

Athens, Greece

Reading's fingernails were embedded in the dash as he held on for dear life, Major Nicolo on the bumper of a squad car blazing a trail through the busy streets that were Athens. Units from around the city were apparently converging on the house discovered by Tommy, and Nicolo was none too pleased about how he had done it.

The major growled at him, still not over the slight. "I should have them arrested."

"They're too rich. One phone call and any charges you managed to come up with would be dropped."

Nicolo growled. "Don't they realize how much time they wasted? We could have contained the situation hours ago, and had her out by now."

"Perhaps. Or they could shoot her the moment they see the first flashing light."

"We have expert hostage negotiators. They would have been able to end this peacefully."

Reading shook his head. "You're dealing with the Suqut Brigade. These are fanatics. These people will never surrender. All we should be focusing on is Professor Galanos' safe return."

Nicolo shook his head then cranked the wheel, sending them careening around a corner. "If they're fanatics, then how do you propose we get them to give her up?"

Reading frowned. "I'm afraid the only way might be an armed assault, but the only way that will work is if we plan it carefully. There can't be too many of them in there, not after so many were killed at the dig site."

"How many have your friends seen on camera?"

"As far as I know, only the leader. My partner has identified him as Ahmed Rafiq. A true fanatic."

"Well, I've got snipers on the way. If we're lucky, we might be able to take most of them out."

Reading chewed his cheek for a moment, an idea occurring to him when his phone rang. He checked the display then took the call. "Jim, we're still en route."

"How much longer?"

Reading looked at Nicolo. "ETA?"

"Five minutes."

Reading returned to the call. "Five minutes."

"They just shot the man they were holding. He's dead."

"And the professor's wife?"

"She's still alive. The leader just got a call."

"What's being said?"

"I don't know. They discovered the camera in the room they're gathering in, so we can't hear anything there anymore. You have to hurry, Hugh, it looks like they might kill her, depending on what's said in that phone call."

Reading turned to Nicolo. "We might not have five minutes."

Outside the Suqut Brigade Safe House

Athens, Greece

"You wanted to talk?"

Utkin pointed at the screen, facial recognition analysis of the footage captured earlier confirming the identity of the man Tankov was talking to. Ahmed Rafiq. A psychotic bastard if there ever was one.

It will be a pleasure to kill you.

"I want to deal."

"But, Rafiq, my friend, you have nothing I want."

There was a pause, and Tankov wished he could see the man's face. "So, you know my name."

"I do."

"It changes nothing."

Tankov grunted. "For you perhaps. For me? It means I control the situation completely."

"I still have the professor's wife."

Tankov shrugged. "What do I care?"

"So, you don't work for the professor?"

Tankov smiled. "I think you know who I work for."

Another pause. "Sheik Khalid."

"Exactly. He's very disappointed that you tried to double-cross him."

"But we didn't! We never had it. You know that!"

Tankov decided to have some fun. "How do I know that?"

"Because you have the damned artifact!"

"I do?"

Rafiq growled. "Don't play stupid with me. My man saw you hit the dig site. It was in the trunk of a car."

Tankov made a mental note to see if he could track down the other man.

Just to be thorough.

"Well, if I have it, then I'll be in the sheik's good graces." He winked at Utkin. "Gee, I'd hate to be in your shoes."

"I'll pay you to tell him the truth. That's all I'm asking. Tell him the truth. Tell him that we never had it, that we never double-crossed him, and I'll make it worth your while."

Tankov loved the desperation now in the man's voice. It meant he was ready to panic. "I don't need money."

"I'll give you the woman."

"I don't need women. Kill her or don't kill her. It makes no difference to me. When we arrive, you're all dead anyway."

He ended the call, tossing his phone on the workstation that extended along the entire left side of the van. "That should get him panicking." He motioned at the displays. "Play back the fence getting shot. He said something just before he bought it."

Utkin brought up the footage. Tankov watched, listening carefully. "What do you think he was about to say?"

"What? About who he knows?"

"Yeah. But I know who..." He paused, thinking about the possibilities. "I know who has it?"

Utkin shook his head. "No, that would mean he knows us."

"Or he's mistaken in who he thinks has it."

"He was lying in order to save his life?"

Tankov scratched his chin. "Wait, bring up the footage where they took the woman to the bathroom."

"Her room or his?"

"His."

Utkin worked the controls, backing up the footage for both feeds until it showed her taken from the room. "Here we go."

"Zoom in on his face. I noticed it earlier, but didn't think much of it at the time." He pointed at the screen as Damos' jaw dropped. "See, he was surprised at something he saw."

Utkin shrugged. "The only thing happening at the time was the woman being taken to the bathroom."

Tankov nodded. "Exactly. How much do you want to bet that they walked her right past his room, and he recognized her?"

"Yeah, and he looked pretty angry after he saw whatever it was he saw."

Tankov agreed. "Right. Surprised then angry. And then, just before they shoot him, he says, what was it?"

"Wait, there's something I have to tell you, or something like that."

"Exactly. Then he says, 'but I know who.' I bet you that he was going to say something like, 'but I know who she is,' or something to that effect."

Utkin's eyes narrowed. "But how does he know her? Were they having an affair or something?"

Tankov smacked him on the back of his head. "This isn't a romance novel. She's involved! She has to be!" He leaned back in his chair. "It has to be her. It makes perfect sense."

"I'm lost."

"Of course you are. You were artillery. Leave the thinking to the real soldiers."

Utkin gave him the finger. "I was artillery for six months. I served ten years."

"Six months is enough. The damage was done."

"Haha. So, are you going to fill me in?"

Tankov pointed at the feed from the camera on the roof of the truck, positioned to monitor the street and the front of the house. "We've got activity." He activated his comm, connecting to the rest of the team. "They're leaving now." He glanced at the camera showing the live feed of the woman's room. It was empty. "It looks like they're taking the female hostage with them. Let's try not to kill her. She's innocent in all this."

Though he wasn't so sure about that anymore.

Reading pried his fingernails from the dash and climbed out of the car, quickly taking in the scene before him, this apparently one of two staging areas, the other on the opposite end of the street where their hostage-takers were located. Dozens of police were rushing about, a roadblock already set up, a tactical team readying their gear.

This isn't going to end well.

He followed Nicolo, wishing he spoke Greek, instead relying on his decades of experience to guess what they were going to do.

Nicolo cursed, enough concern on his face to have Reading poking his nose into the conversation.

"What?"

"They're leaving the premises."

Reading cursed, grabbing a pair of binoculars from one of the more junior men. He headed for the corner and peered around the building, spotting four hostiles and a woman.

Professor Galanos.

He turned back to Nicolo. "Are your snipers in position?"

Nicolo shook his head. "Not yet."

Reading cursed again. "Then this is going to get ugly, quickly."

"We'll box them in and take them by force. We'll have two dozen weapons on them in seconds."

Reading shook his head. "That won't work with these people. They want to die by the infidel's hand. If you try to arrest them, they'll open fire. Your only hope is to take them all out at once."

Nicolo joined the cursing. "But we're not ready."

A squad car screamed onto the scene, lights and sirens blazing, a young officer stumbling out, clearly a bundle of nerves. Everyone turned, shouting at him, and his aghast expression confirmed he understood the mistake he had made.

Reading peered down the block, the hostiles staring in his direction.

"We've been made."

"The cops are here."

Tankov cursed and activated his comm. "Okay, everybody fall back to Point Bravo." He climbed into the van with two of the others, Utkin already at the wheel. Tankov sat in the passenger seat, peeling off his body armor and other accouterments of the trade, the guys in the back stowing it in hidden compartments as the displays and workstations flipped, replaced by fully-stocked tool cabinets.

They were now a commercial HVAC maintenance crew.

"Remember, calmly, slowly. There's probably going to be a roadblock."

Utkin glanced in his side mirror. "The hostiles are on the street with the woman. It looks like they're debating whether or not to go back into the house."

"Let's not worry about that. Either way, they're not going anywhere. Between the kidnappings and the murders, if they survive the next ten minutes, they're going to prison for a long time. That should satisfy the client. If he wants, he can have them killed on the inside."

They rounded a bend in the street and Tankov cautioned the others with a muttered warning, no lips moved. "Everyone stay calm, but no stupid grins. We're just friendly Russian immigrants on our way home after a tough day on the job."

But it didn't matter.

They were waved through, the officers manning the barricade quickly moving it aside and impatiently urging them onward. Tankov gave the man nearest him a friendly nod as Utkin gently pressed on the gas, sending them through the cordon of police and back into the peaceful though questionable neighborhood.

"That was easy."

Utkin grinned. "I have a trustworthy face."

"What's our range on the cameras?"

Utkin took a right, evidently anticipating where the question was leading. "We should be able to pick them up two streets over."

"Do it. I want to see what happens so we can report, rather than have our client read about it in tomorrow's paper."

Utkin guided them into a parking spot moments later, the guys in the back already having reactivated the equipment. "I've got the signals."

Tankov took his seat in the back, the two remaining cameras showing only empty rooms. "Send in a drone."

Utkin opened one of the drawers behind him and pointed, Vasiliev grabbing the case inside. In less than a minute, the drone was deployed, and they all watched as Vasiliev guided it into position over the street they had just left, high enough to give them a full view of both police positions and the hostiles.

Hostiles who had evidently decided not to return to the house.

Muzzle flashes erupted from one of their weapons, the distinct sound of automatic gunfire reaching their ears two streets over.

He frowned, thinking of the woman with them.

And the grad student languishing in jail for a crime he wasn't certain she committed.

King George Hotel

Athens, Greece

They were in the dark. The two camera feeds they still had access to showed empty rooms, and Reading had passed on Major Nicolo's orders to get the drone they were using out of his sky. Tommy had instead suggested they simply land it on the roof of a nearby building so it wouldn't be in the way, and they had all agreed.

But it left them with the view of a rooftop, and nothing else except muffled audio.

"I've got another camera signal. Patching it through now." Tommy pointed at the screen and they all gathered around the television.

Acton tried to make sense of what they were looking at. "What is that?"

Adelaide, an expert in these things as Leather had finally revealed to them, explained as she pointed at various things on the image. "On either side here, we have police positions. They're obviously not concerned about being spotted since they have their lights going."

Acton's eyes narrowed. "That seems odd."

"I'm guessing they were spotted." She pointed at the center of the screen. "These must be our hostiles, and"—she pointed at a figure held by one of them—"this is probably Professor Galanos."

"Juno," whispered Antoniou, his eyes glued to the screen.

Acton squeezed the man's shoulder. "She's still alive. That's good news."

Antoniou nodded, then gasped as gunfire erupted from one of the hostiles, the muzzle flash lighting up the darkened street. "Juno!"

Outside the Suqut Brigade Safe House
Athens, Greece

Reading cursed as gunfire rang out from the officers manning this end of the street, an entirely incorrect response to the situation. They should have remained behind their cover, and let the hostiles waste their ammo as the snipers continued to get into position.

Yet that wasn't at all what was happening.

He searched for Nicolo in the throng of officers, but couldn't find him, the major probably behind one of the dozen or more vehicles crammed into the area. Reading poked his head up from the retaining wall he was positioned behind, then immediately dropped as a barrage of lead was sent his way. An officer cried out five paces to his left, falling backward, blood oozing from a wound to the arm. Reading crawled over and pulled him behind the wall, checking the wound.

"Medic!"

He had no clue if anyone would understand him, so he instead yanked the man's belt off and used it as a tourniquet on the gushing wound.

"I need a medic over here!"

Two paramedics with a backboard suddenly rounded a van. They dropped, crawling the rest of the way, then with Reading's help, lifted the wounded man onto the more portable stretcher.

He was gone within what felt like far too long to Reading, but was likely less than two minutes.

And the gunfire showed no signs of abating from either side.

She's going to die, if she hasn't already.

Rafiq emptied his magazine, grunting with satisfaction as yet another infidel police officer went down. *This* was what he had always wanted. *This* was how he had always wanted to die.

In battle.

Against infidels.

This wasn't the execution he had feared, the unsatisfying ending that only minutes before was his future. This was a battle against the forces that would dare oppose Islam's foretold domination of Allah's dominion.

Dying here today, in the name of Allah, would guarantee him entry into paradise, entry into Jannah.

He smiled at the others. "Allahu Akbar!"

He shoved his body against the woman's, pinning her to the car as he reloaded, then as he moved back and reached for her, she kneed him in the balls and dropped to the ground.

"You bitch!" He pointed his gun at her head and squeezed the trigger as she rolled under the vehicle.

Antoniou cried out as he watched the man who had held his wife fire into the pavement, and they all held their collective breath, leaning closer to the screen, searching for Juno in the dark, but not finding her.

"Where'd she go?" asked Mai, voicing the question they all had on their lips.

Acton shook his head. "I think she went under the car."

"Oh no!" cried Laura, pointing as the man dropped to a knee, swinging his weapon under the vehicle. "He's going after her!"

"Please, God, no!" sobbed Antoniou, tears flowing down his cheeks as he helplessly watched the events rapidly unfolding miles away, and likely the final moments of his beloved wife's life.

Tankov frowned as he watched Rafiq about to eliminate the woman. "That's unfortunate."

Utkin agreed. "Too bad we weren't the ones in there. They'd all be dead already, and she'd be alive."

Tankov shook his head. "This operation was botched the moment they were made. They obviously don't have any snipers in place, and the guys returning fire can't seem to hit anything. All four hostiles are still in the fight." He spat. "Amateurs."

One of the hostiles dropped, making a liar out of him.

Utkin grinned.

Reading peered out from his position and smiled as one of the hostiles was finally taken out, leaving three to deal with, and what he hoped was a dwindling supply of ammunition. But it was Juno that was his concern, and he couldn't see her.

"Where's the hostage?" asked Nicolo as he rushed up beside him. "I lost sight of her."

Reading glanced at the missing major then resumed watching the battle unfold. "I don't know. They're all between parked cars, so I can't see. She's not in the street or on the sidewalk, so she must be on the ground between them."

"So, she could be dead."

"Let's hope not, but yes. You have to get your men to stop shooting. We need to negotiate our way out of this."

Nicolo shook his head. "Didn't you hear what they were all just yelling?"

Reading frowned. He had. Allahu Akbar. God is greater. The rallying cry for jihadists everywhere. These men were every bit the fundamentalists he had been told, and this was their chance for entry into their twisted paradise should they die in jihad against the infidels like him.

He sighed, Nicolo absolutely correct. "Where are the snipers?"

"Getting into position now. This should be over in a couple of minutes."

270

"Let's hope she lasts that long."

"Drop the drone down. I want to see her."

Utkin glanced at Tankov. "Are you sure? I'd have to land the damned thing. It could get hit, and will definitely be noticed."

"Do it. I need to know if she's alive."

Utkin sighed. "If we lose the drone, it's coming out of your share."

Everyone chuckled, even Tankov, as the drone rapidly dropped to the ground, the image turning from a bird's eye view of the battle, to an up close and personal shot of the pavement. The camera panned and suddenly they were looking at a shot across the street, at ground level, the woman clearly visible under one of the vehicles, Rafiq on one side lowering himself to get at her, and the body of one of the Brigade members lying in a heap on the other.

"She's got about five seconds, I'd say."

Tankov growled. "Where the hell are their snipers? This is ridiculous!" He pointed at Vasiliev. "Take a sniper rifle and see if you can get a shot."

Vasiliev nodded, grabbing the weapon and hopping out the back of the van.

Utkin frowned. "I don't think he'll get there in time."

Tankov sighed. "Neither do I."

Acton's eyes narrowed in confusion as the image changed, showing them nothing but pavement. "Did it get shot down?"

Tommy shook his head. "I don't think so, that was a controlled descent."

Adelaide pointed as the angle changed. "Look. Is that Professor Galanos?"

Antoniou was jubilant. "It is! She's still alive!"

Acton frowned as the terrorist, now prone, repositioned his weapon. He put a hand on Antoniou's shoulder. "Basil, you may not want to watch this."

Antoniou shook his head. "I-I have to. She's my wife. She's all I have."

Laura gasped out a cry as the weapon dragged across the pavement, and Acton closed his eyes, praying for someone to save the woman before it was too late.

Adelaide shot to her feet. "Look!"

Rafiq dropped to the ground, staring into the woman's eyes as he swung his weapon toward her. He would be dead soon, and that pleased him to no end. But he couldn't let the opportunity to kill one last infidel woman pass him by. And as he stared at her one final time, the events of the past two days played themselves out once more, and it gave him pause.

Damos had said his contact was a woman, and that she worked on the inside. The artifact was found in the trunk of a car at the dig site, which meant it had been hidden there during their attack. Damos' contact had been the one who told them when to attack, so she would have been ready to hand over the artifact, and when things went wrong, she would have been forced to hide it somewhere.

But why hide it in her own vehicle? The area was bound to be searched eventually, the artifact found, and she'd be arrested.

He smiled at her. "It was you all along."

She nodded. "I had to help my husband." She swiftly reached out behind her, grabbing a pistol from the hand of Zaman, dead behind her. His heart hammered and he swung his weapon, the muzzle catching on the rear tire, giving her time to aim Zaman's gun at his head. "I'm sorry. No one was supposed to get hurt."

She squeezed the trigger, cutting off Rafiq's prayer for entry into Jannah.

Utkin pointed at the screen, bouncing in his chair. "Did she just shoot him?"

Tankov leaned back, smiling. "I think so."

"Man, that is *definitely* my kind of woman."

Tankov grunted. "You'd be wise to remain cautious around a woman like that. The way you are with them, you're liable to provoke the exact same reaction."

Utkin and the others laughed, then he suddenly became serious, sitting upright in his chair. "Wait a sec."

Tankov leaned closer, his eyes narrowing at his man's concerned expression. "What?"

"Somebody's tapped our camera feeds."

Tankov's eyebrows rose. "Are you sure?"

Utkin pointed at one of the technical displays. "Yes. Someone else is connected to our network."

Tankov frowned. "How'd they manage that? I thought this stuff was secure."

"It is. Normally. But, well…"

Tankov sensed he was about to get pissed off. "What?"

"Well, I had to reset this damned thing at the hotel, and there wasn't time to update it with the latest BIOS. Obviously, there was some sort of security hole that they tapped."

Tankov wasn't sure he bought the explanation. "And they just thought to look for it?"

Utkin glanced over his shoulder at him as he worked the keyboard. "Any hacker worth his salt will try the known vulnerabilities first, because most people don't install their updates, especially hardware updates."

Tankov exhaled loudly. "How long have they been connected?"

Utkin cursed. "Pretty much since we set up the feeds."

"Unbelievable. Who?"

Utkin shrugged. "Our Brigade friends?"

Tankov shook his head. "No, they'd have been going apeshit, and they were genuinely surprised when they found the camera we meant for them to find."

"Police?"

"Possible, but if it was them, then why did they wait so long? It's been hours. And how could they have found the place so quickly? We only found it because we followed Damos."

Utkin turned in his chair. "Could they have been watching him too?"

Tankov's head bobbed. "Possible, but again, why wait so long to hit the place? They kept investigating as if they had no clue where she was or who was even involved."

Utkin scratched his chin then tapped it. "Yeah, and we kept sweeping the neighborhood. We'd have spotted a police operation."

"Not necessarily. They could be monitoring from across the city for all we know."

Utkin shook his head. "No, whoever is doing this is here, now."

Tankov's eyebrows shot up. "What?"

Utkin gestured at their gear. "We're not exactly broadcasting across the Internet here. We're sending signals from our cameras connected to our own private router, sitting in this van. Think Bluetooth rather than cellular. You have to be close to be connected."

"So, they were here all along?"

"Yes, or…"

Tankov eyed Utkin. "What?"

"Did anyone spot a drone hovering about?"

Vasiliev's voice came in over the gear, their conversation shared among the team. "I thought I heard something earlier, but I thought it was just some kids playing."

Utkin rapped his knuckles on the workstation. "That's how I'd do it. Send in a drone with a cellular connection to the Internet, tap our signals, then transmit the footage to wherever I am."

Tankov chewed his cheek. "But they'd still have to have known where to send the drone."

"Well, we know they were sending text messages to the woman's husband. Do you think he'd have gone to the police?"

Tankov shook his head. "I wouldn't have." A smile spread across his face. "But I think I know exactly who we're dealing with." He motioned at the camera footage. "Can you override what they see?"

"Absolutely."

Only two remained, yet they seemed to have an endless supply of ammo, Reading having spotted them reaching into the back seat of a vehicle on several occasions. He had no angle on Juno, and for all he knew, she was dead, but the sooner this was over, the more chances she had to survive if it weren't so.

A loud shot cracked out, heard above everything else going on, and Reading breathed a sigh of relief as the sniper round took out one of the two remaining men. A moment later, another shot rang out, and the final man dropped, the gunfire dwindling to nothing within moments.

"Tactical teams, advance!"

Reading stood, still keeping a wary eye on things in case one of the hostiles was just wounded, and watched as tactical teams from both ends of the street rushed forward, their weapons trained on the bloody scene before them.

Nicolo came up beside him, watching through binoculars, shaking his head as if confused.

"Your sniper teams did a good job."

Nicolo shook his head. "Thanks, but there's just one problem."

Reading's eyes narrowed. "What's that?"

"They're not in position yet."

King George Hotel

Athens, Greece

"There she is!" cried Antoniou, pointing at the screen, his wife crawling out from under the car, the gunfire they had been hearing silenced. Black boots filled the screen, then men knelt beside her, revealing their police uniforms as they helped her to her feet. Hugs rounded the room as tears of joy and relief flowed without shame, even Leather, still at the door, glistening.

Acton's phone rang and he answered it without looking, unable to tear his eyes from the screen. "Hello?"

"Hey, Jim, it's me."

"Just a sec, Hugh, I'll put you on speaker." Acton tapped the display, and everyone cocked an ear, though kept their eyes on the screen.

"Tell Professor Antoniou she's safe. We have her."

Antoniou glanced at the phone, clasping his hands to his chest in thanks, then resumed his vigil. Acton grinned. "Way ahead of you. We watched the entire thing."

"How? I thought the cameras were inside?"

"Whoever is doing this launched a drone. We watched the whole thing. If you look, it's probably sitting on the street not ten feet from where Juno was hiding."

"I'll check it out."

"Okay, we're going to head there now. I don't think Basil can wait."

"That might not be a good idea."

The video went black. "Wait, we just lost the feed." A message appeared on the screen. "What the hell?"

"What's going on?"

"The video feed has been replaced by a message."

"What does it say?"

Acton's chest tightened as he read the white on black message. "I know you're watching, Professor Acton. Meet me in thirty minutes. Alone." He drew a quick breath as everyone stared at him. "There's a set of GPS coordinates."

Tommy tapped at his keyboard then swung the laptop around. "It's the National Garden. About twenty minutes from here."

"Then I don't have much time."

Reading cursed. "That's the idea. It gives you no time to think."

"But I have to know what this is about."

Laura stared at him, wide-eyed. "You're not going to meet with them!"

"Why not?"

"I can think of a thousand reasons why not."

Reading growled. "And I can think of a thousand more. How about we start with the fact we don't know who *they* are."

Acton pursed his lips. "There's only one way to find out. They have to be the ones who have Cylon's urn. Maybe they want to return it."

"Why the bloody hell would they want to do that?"

Acton shrugged. "I don't know. Buyer's remorse?"

Antoniou shook his head. "My wife is safe. There's no reason for anyone to put themselves at risk anymore. It's just an artifact. It's not worth dying for."

Laura patted the man on the knee. "I agree."

"I don't think they mean to harm me."

A burst of static erupted from the phone. "Are you clairvoyant now?"

Acton chuckled. "Think about it. This Suqut Brigade is now dead. We know the message isn't coming from them, it's coming from the group that was watching them."

"Right, the same group that shot up the dig site a few hours ago, and put some Taser thing in my chest."

"Exactly. They didn't kill you. And you said the man knew me."

"They didn't kill me, but they wounded some of the others."

"Only because they fought back."

Antoniou shook his head. "You're defending these people!"

Acton's eyes widened at the misunderstanding. "No, not at all! Hear me out. This Suqut Brigade attacked the site, killed some innocent people, and a bunch of them were killed. This other group tried not to kill people. I agree, this is horrible, and they should all go to jail for the rest of their lives. But they didn't even try to kill Hugh or anybody else they didn't have to. That means they went in with the intent of not killing. There's no reason to think these people mean me any harm, and there's every reason to believe they have the artifact. They might have retrieved it for any number of reasons, and maybe that reason fell through. That could mean they're willing to give it back."

Reading was having none of it. "This is insane."

"I agree, but we need to know who was behind all this."

Laura stared at him, shaking her head. "But we do know. The Suqut Brigade."

Acton shook his head. "No, I mean the inside person."

"And we know that. Cy Pulos."

Acton frowned. "I'm not so sure about that."

Antoniou's eyebrows shot up. "What do you mean? They found it in her car."

Acton jabbed at the air between them. "Exactly! Why would she put it in her own car trunk? It makes no sense. She had to know that it could be searched eventually, and it would point directly at her."

Laura still wasn't on his side. "She might not have had a choice. Bullets were flying everywhere. She would be in a hurry, probably a panic."

Acton shook his head. "You're forgetting one thing. She knew they were coming. She was expecting the bullets. She would have taken it to exactly where they had agreed to exchange it, and would likely have had a backup plan because of Korba's men being there. I think whoever took it never intended to put it in Cy's car, but when things went wrong, decided it was time to go to Plan B."

Antoniou's head slowly bobbed. "We did have a custom of leaving all the cars unlocked. Too many car alarms kept going off. It would be an easy thing to just reach in and pop a trunk."

Laura looked at him. "Don't tell me you're buying into this now?"

Acton reached out and took her hand. "I think she's being framed."

Laura sighed, staring into his eyes, worry written in the creases around her eyes. "By whom?"

"I'm not sure, but maybe these guys can tell us. They knew about the car too. We still have questions that need to be answered, and they might be the only ones with those answers."

"But why risk your life?"

"I'm not. Something else is going on here. That message is directed at me specifically. Why? Why not you, Basil? Or a generic 'you?' How did they know it was *me* that was watching, and why do they want to speak to *me*?" He shook his head. "No, there's something more going on here, and I intend to find out what."

Laura stared at him, her eyes wide. "You're mad!"

He chuckled. "Madly curious, but not mad."

"Then I'm going with you."

"*You're* mad."

Leather stepped forward. "If she's going, I'm going."

Acton rose, checking the time, precious minutes having ticked away. "No, nobody's going except me. They said alone. If anyone else shows up, then things could go south quickly."

Laura stood beside him. "There's no talking you out of this, is there?"

"No." He looked at Leather. "I need a car."

Adelaide tossed a set of keys at him. "I rented one." She shrugged. "I was bored." Her jaw dropped, aghast at what she had just said. "I'm sorry, hon, I didn't mean it that way."

Leather smiled. "We'll discuss how I bore you later." He looked at Acton. "We should wire you."

Reading replied. "Absolutely not. They obviously know you have the ability to tap into their signals. They'll be looking for anything out of the ordinary. If you're going to be a moron and do this, then do it right and follow their instructions to the letter. And if you get yourself killed, I'll beat the living daylights out of you the next time I see you."

Acton grinned. "That could get you kicked out of wherever I'm going."

"Don't be so sure that's where you'll end up."

Acton laughed and gave Laura a hug. "Wish me luck."

"You're an idiot," she whispered, tears in her eyes. She gave him a gentle kiss. "Don't die on me."

His chest tightened as he was about to depart on what was, a moment ago, merely an idea. "I'll try not to."

Outside the Suqut Brigade Safe House

Athens, Greece

Reading ended the call, cursing the stupidity of his friend, though he understood the reasoning. Acton was a man who had to have all the answers. He was the same way. And Acton's logic was sound, though Reading didn't think it was worth betting his life on. He had no idea who the second team was, but there was one piece of information he hadn't revealed to Acton and the others as it would have just encouraged his friend.

Someone had intervened here, ending the standoff, and likely saving Juno's life.

That someone had to be the same people who had positioned the cameras, and because they had sent their message directly to Acton, and the second team that had hit the dig site also claimed to know him, they had to be one and the same.

There was no way he was about to believe a third team was involved.

If they were truly bad people, why help save the wife?

I wish I was going with him.

He walked over to Major Nicolo as he spoke to Juno, the woman being tended to by a paramedic, appearing in reasonable condition, though she had clearly been punched in the face at some point.

Nicolo looked at him, then held out a hand. "Professor, may I introduce Agent Hugh Reading of Interpol. My understanding is that he is good friends with Professors Acton and Palmer."

Juno's eyes widened at the mention of their names. "Have you spoken to my husband?"

"I just told him the good news. He wanted to come here, but I told him not to, just in case the area isn't secure. You'll see him very soon, don't worry."

Her shoulders slumped and she sighed, eyeing a gurney with a body bag being pushed past. "How did you find me?"

Reading exchanged a quick glance with Nicolo, then replied. "An anonymous tip."

"Thank God." She reached out, grabbing his forearm. "Did you find it? Cylon's urn?"

Reading nodded. "We did."

She sucked in a quick breath, her eyes wide, then exhaled slowly. "Thank God. I feared the worst. These men kept insisting my husband had it."

"He didn't. Unfortunately, the urn was stolen before we could secure it."

Her eyes narrowed. "By these…men?"

Reading shook his head. "No, we think it was another group."

"My God! How many people are after it?"

"At least three, by the looks of it."

Her eyes narrowed. "Three? Who's the third?"

"Your grad student, Cy Pulos. We arrested her earlier for stealing artifacts from the dig site."

"Impossible!"

"We found them in her apartment. And we found the urn in the trunk of her car."

Juno shook her head. "She's such a wonderful student." She squared her jaw. "I don't believe it for a second."

Reading eyed her. "Neither do I."

The National Garden

Athens, Greece

Acton stepped out of the car, taking a moment to enjoy the view surrounding him. He had never been here before, though from what little he could see from the street lights, it was beautiful. The greenery on the other side of the gates signaled an oasis from the chaos of modern life. He would have to come here with Laura at some point, to take it all in.

But he had a specific purpose today, and was already two minutes late.

He approached the closed gates, nobody in sight, and frowned.

Am I supposed to climb the fence?

On a whim, he tried the handle, and the gate swung open.

Immediately raising the hairs on the back of his neck, for once he entered, he was absolutely alone with whoever had brought him here.

He committed, and walked deeper into the garden when a voice echoed from the shadows.

"That's far enough, Professor Acton."

Acton stopped, his heart hammering, though happy to have heard words rather than gunshots upon his arrival. "Okay, I'm here. What do you want?"

"To talk."

Acton's eyes narrowed. "About?"

"About the truth."

"Who are you? Hugh said that you claimed to know me."

"I'm someone you wouldn't recognize."

Acton took a chance. "Then why not show yourself?"

A figure stepped out of the shadows, though only his silhouette was revealed, his face still obscured.

"I can't see your face."

There was a chuckle. "It wouldn't matter. Like I said, you wouldn't recognize me."

Acton tensed, something familiar about the voice. "But I know you, don't I?"

"Yes, Professor Acton, you know me."

His heart hammered, now certain he knew the voice.

Yet he couldn't place it.

If only I could see his face.

Yet the man insisted he wouldn't recognize him. What did that mean? Was it someone he had only ever heard on the phone?

"You're aware that Professor Antoniou's wife was successfully rescued."

"I am." He smiled slightly. "And the fact that you are aware, means you were somehow involved."

"We were, though not with the kidnapping."

"No, but you stole Cylon's urn."

"We did in the end."

"Where is it now?"

"Somewhere safe."

Acton shook his head. "It will only be safe if it is returned."

"Not true, Professor, not true. There are collectors who will take very good care of it."

"So, you're thieves."

Another chuckle. "I prefer to think of us as precious artifact acquisition experts."

Acton grunted. "You can put lipstick on a pig, but it's still a pig."

"I don't know what that means."

Acton paused, peering into the shadows. "Your voice. I know it from somewhere. You say we know each other. From where?"

"If I told you everything, what would be the fun in that?"

Acton was getting frustrated. "Then why am I here?"

"Let's just say that we have turned over a new leaf."

Acton frowned. "Something tells me you don't know what that means either."

Laughter rolled across the garden. "This one, I do."

"Then again, why am I here?"

"As I said, to discuss the truth."

"Then please, tell me what truth you're talking about."

"The police have arrested a graduate student named Cy Pulos for the thefts."

Acton's stomach flipped, finally realizing why he was here. "Yes."

"Are you convinced she's behind everything?"

Acton paused, debating on what his answer should be. He decided truth was the way to go. "No, I don't."

"Then who do you think is behind it?"

Acton pursed his lips, staring at the silhouette, deciding the complete truth wouldn't necessarily be wise. "I hesitate to say, but I have a feeling you're about to tell me."

The man chuckled. "I've missed you, Professor." He took a step closer, his face still lost in the shadows. "If I were the young woman's lawyer, I'd be asking what Professor Antoniou's wife was doing during the attack on the dig site."

Acton pulled in a quick breath, his heart hammering. "Why do you say that?"

"Watch the footage you tapped into, carefully. All of it. I think you'll be able to figure it out."

Yet he already knew what the man was talking about. The fence had recognized somebody, and it could only have been Juno. They knew from the overheard conversations between the Brigade members that the inside person was a woman.

And he had never believed that the grad student would have been stupid enough to put the urn in her own trunk.

It had to be Juno, and the very idea was sickening, so much so that he couldn't believe it.

Yet it had to be.

But how could he prove it? The footage wouldn't be enough. A man reacting to something seen off camera meant little, and that man was now dead. Juno would deny it, and Cy had the artifact in her trunk, and even more at her apartment.

"I need proof."

"I have it. My client had a recording of a meeting between his contact, and the woman on the inside. I'm confident that this conversation is between Karan Damos, the other man who had been taken hostage, and Professor Galanos."

Acton felt faint. "Do you have this recording?"

"I do."

"And you can hear her voice on it?"

"Yes. You should be able to perform voice recognition analysis on it and confirm the identity."

Acton drew a quick breath. "And you're going to give me this recording?"

The silhouette bent over and a cellphone slid from the shadows, coming to rest at Acton's feet. He picked it up. "It's on here?"

"Yes."

The man turned and began to walk away. "Say hello to your wife for me."

Acton's eyes narrowed. The man had met both of them, yet they wouldn't recognize him if they saw his face. He spoke excellent English, but wasn't American. A special ops type team had hit the dig site.

His stomach flipped as he finally recognized the voice.

And it terrified him.

Yet he couldn't resist confirming it.

"You're the one who stole the Amber Room."

The silhouette stopped then turned back to face him. "So, you've finally figured it out."

Rage mixed with the terror he felt. "Where is it?"

The man took a step closer. "You expect me to tell you?"

"You've turned over a new leaf, haven't you?"

The man laughed. "You know what, Professor, I'm feeling generous." A finger was raised. "To a point. My employer betrayed me by giving an easy job to butchers. People died, and there was no need for that. I think he deserves to suffer a little, don't you?"

Acton tried to control the giddiness he now felt. Could he be about to find out where the fabled Amber Room had ended up? He inhaled deeply. "I do."

"Then follow the phone."

And with that, the man turned, disappearing into the shadows, his footfalls fading to nothing.

Leaving Acton to wonder what he could possibly mean.

King George Hotel

Athens, Greece

Acton forced a smile as he entered the hotel room, a happy reunion taking place between Juno and her husband. Laura rushed into his arms, hugging him hard.

"Thank you for not getting yourself killed."

He smiled. "You're welcome."

"So, what was it all about? You didn't really say anything when you called."

"Give me a moment, will you? I'm still a little wound up."

"Then you need champagne!" cried Antoniou, bringing him a glass then giving him a thumping hug. "Thank you for saving my wife!"

Acton smiled, holding up his glass in acknowledgment, though not taking a drink. "I think we should be thanking Tommy. If it weren't for him, we never would have been able to track down where Juno was, or monitor the cameras."

A round of cheers went up for Tommy, who blushed, then blushed even further when a proud Mai gave him a kiss that had the room urging them on. Finally freed of his partner, Acton motioned for him to join him near the door.

"What is it, Professor?"

Acton handed him the phone given him earlier. "There's an audio recording on this between a man and a woman. Retrieve it, and let me know when you've got it." He stared into the young man's eyes, emphasizing his next point. "Make sure you don't damage it. We're going to need to track everywhere it's been."

"Consider it done." Tommy grabbed his laptop, disappearing into the bedroom, Mai following him.

Acton had had almost half an hour to think about what the man said. Follow the phone. It hadn't made any sense to him at first, but as he thought about it with the clarity that only came from calm, he realized the man had to have meant for him to track the phone.

He could only pray that he was right, for if he were, he had a feeling the phone would lead them to one of the greatest stolen pieces of art of all time.

Reading walked over to him, drink in hand. "So, you're alive."

"I am."

"Are you going to tell us what happened?"

"Give me a couple of minutes." Tommy reappeared, nodding. "Make that a few seconds." He leaned closer to Reading, lowering his voice. "Mind the door, would you?"

Reading's eyes narrowed, but he said nothing, instead walking casually to the no longer guarded door.

Acton stepped into the middle of the boisterous group, noting Major Nicolo sitting near the window, probably wondering why Acton had asked Reading to make sure he was there when he arrived. He raised his hands slightly, quieting everyone. "Okay, I think we're ready to clear this up."

The seriousness of his tone had everyone settling down immediately.

"Tommy, can you play it on the big screen so everyone can hear it through its speakers?"

Tommy's tone was muted. "Yes, sir."

Acton turned to the room, keeping Juno in sight, though not staring at her directly. "What we are about to hear is a recording of a conversation between the fence, Damos, and the person responsible for the previous thefts, and for arranging the theft of Cylon's urn."

If there had been any noise in the room, it was gone now, as everyone turned their attention to the television.

Including a clearly nervous Juno.

Leather headed slowly for the door, apparently picking up on what was going on.

Acton turned to Tommy. "Ready?"

"Yes."

He tapped a key and the audio started, even Acton on edge with anticipation, as he too was hearing it for the first time.

"I have a more valuable item."

"What?"

"An urn, with a curse written by Cylon himself. I'll want seven figures for it."

"That's too rich for me."

Antoniou's jaw dropped. "Wait! I know that voice!" Acton signaled for Tommy to pause the recording as Antoniou turned on his wife. "It's you!"

Juno slowly backed away from her husband, shaking her head. "How could you think such a thing?"

"There's no doubt! I know my own wife's voice!"

Juno's eyes were wide, her chest heaving as her cheeks flushed. She looked from side to side, for some means of escape, finding none. She bolted for the door but both Reading and Leather stopped her, each taking her by an arm and placing her in a chair.

She collapsed, gripping her head in her hands as she sobbed, her shoulders shaking. It was enough to soften Acton's heart, though only slightly. Too many were dead. Too many innocent people were dead. And no matter how he had felt about her even just earlier today, she deserved prison.

For life.

She stared up at her husband. "I'm so sorry! It's true. But you have to believe me, I never meant for anyone to get hurt. It all started so simply. I was at the market and spotted something on a table that shouldn't have been there. I knew it had to have been stolen. I asked the man, Damos, if he had any other items. I fully intended to have him arrested, but then it occurred to me that we had many items, many duplicates of items, that I might be able to sell, then use the money to help with our funding problems."

"Juno!" whispered Antoniou. "What were you thinking?"

"We were desperate! Every night in bed you'd be complaining about the funding, you were stressing out about how we could continue without more money. We were putting our own money in, and it was destroying our lives, destroying our marriage. I did it for you. I did it for *us*. To save our marriage. We were going bankrupt, and you were oblivious to it. And..." Her shoulders shook as she gasped out a cry. "You were losing me," she whispered.

Antoniou dropped to his knees in front of her, his cheeks stained with tears, and grabbed his wife, holding her tight as they both sobbed together. "But why these men, my love? Why these killers?"

She gently pushed away from him, staring at him with bloodshot eyes. "I didn't know. When we found Cylon's urn, with his curse written on it, I knew that this would be worth millions. If I sold it, I would have enough money to keep us going for years." She sighed, her shoulders slumping. "I had no idea the type of men they'd send for it."

Nicolo stepped forward. "Professor Galanos, I'm placing you under arrest. Will you please stand?"

Juno rose, giving her husband one last hug before Nicolo handcuffed her. She turned to the others. "I'm so sorry, so sorry for everything. I didn't mean for any of this to happen."

Acton stepped forward. "And your student, Cy Pulos. Did she have anything to do with this?"

Juno shook her head. "No, nothing. She was telling the truth. I knew she was taking items home with her to process, then bringing them back the next day. In fact, it was when she didn't get caught by anyone else, that I realized I could do the same thing, but sell them."

Antoniou sighed. "So that's where all the anonymous donations were coming from."

"I'm so sorry. I guess now you'll have to give the money back." Her shoulders shook once again. "I've ruined everything. They'll shut us down for sure." She stared into her husband's eyes. "Can you ever forgive me?"

Antoniou stepped forward and gave her one last hug. "I already have."

Nicolo led her out of the room, Antoniou following.

Reading turned to Acton. "I'm going to go with them, just to tie up some loose ends."

Acton nodded. "Let us know when you're done. We'll give you a lift back to London."

Reading chuckled. "You say that like it's a short hop in a car." He sighed. "Sorry, I just don't have any humor left in me."

Acton knew how he felt, and watched his friend leave, Leather securing the door out of habit.

Tommy broke the awkward silence. "You, umm, wanted me to trace where this phone has been?"

Acton's heart drummed with renewed vigor, the events of moments ago pushed aside. "What did you find?"

298

"It's a burner that's been active for about a week, so it hasn't been in too many places, but it has traveled."

Acton's slumped shoulders squared. "Where?"

"Before here, it was in Saudi Arabia, and before that, Monaco, where it was activated. That's it."

Acton smiled at Laura. "Saudi Arabia." He turned back to Tommy. "Where?"

Tommy pointed at the screen and a satellite view from Google appeared showing a red dot outside of Riyadh. He zoomed in and they were soon looking at an impressive estate, a palatial estate, its grounds a vibrant green, in stark contrast to the arid desert surrounding it.

"That has to be the place!"

Laura stared at him. "What are you talking about? What's this all about?"

Acton jabbed a finger at the screen. "I think that's where the Amber Room is!"

Leroux/White Residence, Fairfax Towers

Falls Church, Virginia

"I thought the acting was great, except for that one guy. He just didn't fit the role."

CIA Analyst Supervisor Chris Leroux's eyes narrowed at his best friend's comment. "You mean the guy playing Han Solo?"

CIA Special Agent Dylan Kane shook his head. "No, he was fine once you got past the fact he wasn't Harrison Ford."

Leroux grabbed another slice of sausage and onion Chicago style from the box. "Then who?"

"Chewbacca."

Agent Sherrie White snorted her Pepsi out her nose while Lee Fang, unfamiliar with American pop culture, looked on confused.

"Wasn't he the walking dog?"

Kane laughed, giving his girlfriend a hug. "Actually, George Lucas said his dog was the inspiration for Chewbacca."

"Who's George Lucas?"

Kane gave her a mock glare. "You call yourself my girlfriend? That's it. We *have* to give you a crash course in all that's important. Next weekend, all nine other Star Wars movies, then all thirteen Star Trek, then all six seasons of Battlestar including the original series, then all seventeen seasons of Stargate."

Leroux grinned. "Sounds like a dream."

Sherrie shook her head. "I think I'm scheduled to assassinate someone that weekend."

Fang, a former Chinese Special Forces operative, now in exile, looked at her with envy. "I wish I could come. I think Dylan just booked up the next two years of weekends."

Kane leaned back on the couch and patted his stomach. "Sounds wonderful, doesn't it."

Leroux finished his slice, then took a drag on his drink. "Pizza and sci-fi, with two beautiful women."

Kane chuckled. "Sounds like a nerd's fantasy."

Leroux frowned. "Fantasy is right. In real life, that *never* happens."

Sherrie patted him on the cheek. "And it still won't, hon. Like I said, I'll be off killing someone."

"Who?"

"Anyone, as long as it gets me out of eighteen hours of Star Wars."

"You like it, and you know it."

"Skip the first three, and maybe."

"Episodes four to six? Are you nuts?"

"No, one to three."

Leroux shook his head. "You have so much to learn."

Sherrie smiled. "And I have no intention of learning it." She took another sip. "I will say this. I did enjoy Solo."

Leroux nodded. "So did I. I don't know why it got such bad press. The reviews are actually good, and the movie was fantastic. The effects were amazing, the acting was great, the story was great, awesome twist at the end." He shrugged. "What's not to love?"

"That they didn't digitally alter Harrison Ford and put him in it."

Leroux groaned at Kane's joke. "Can you imagine? That was the only thing I didn't like in Rogue One. They should have just shot her from behind. Showing that digital face was just terrible."

Kane's phone vibrated and he checked the message. "Huh. Secure." He tapped on the display a few times then held the phone up to his face to unlock it. "It's from Professor Acton."

Leroux shook his head. "What now?"

"Let's find out." Kane dialed, putting the call on speaker.

"Hello?"

"Hey, Doc, it's Dylan. You're on speaker with my friends and colleagues, Lee Fang, Chris Leroux, and Sherrie White. Is everything okay?"

"Actually, for once, I'm not in mortal danger."

"Just calling to say hi?"

Acton laughed. "No, I do need something from you."

Kane chuckled. "I thought you might. How can I help?"

"Remember the Amber Room?"

"That big ass gold and amber room that the Nazis stole, you found, then the Russian art thieves stole back?"

"Yes."

"Let me guess. You found it?"

"Possibly."

Kane exchanged an excited glance with Leroux, and Leroux knew why. Neither of them liked a mission failure, and when they were tricked into thinking the Amber Room was aboard a ship, when all along it wasn't, they had failed in retrieving it.

A black mark on all their records.

"Where is it?"

"Outside Riyadh. I've got exact GPS coordinates I can send you."

"Send them to my secure email."

"Will do. Do you think you can retrieve it?"

Kane shook his head. "In Saudi Arabia? No chance."

The disappointment was clear in Acton's voice. "But we have to do something."

Kane nodded. "Let us discuss it. I'll get back to you."

"All right. Please, Dylan, you have to do something. This thing is priceless, and shouldn't be in some thief's private collection."

"I'll call you back." Kane ended the call then leaned forward. "So, how do we retrieve it?"

Leroux shrugged. "Well, we can't go in. That would cause an international incident that could destabilize the entire region if we were caught."

Sherrie placed the crust of her slice back on her plate then wiped her mouth with her napkin. "If we can't go in to get it, then we have to have it come out."

Kane's eyes narrowed. "You mean make them move it out of the country?"

"Exactly."

"How?"

Sherrie smiled. "By making them *think* we're coming for it."

Kane grinned. "I like it!"

Outside Riyadh, Kingdom of Saudi Arabia

Tankov stared at the urn that had been the cause of so much pain and suffering—with an intact lid its new owner had no intention of opening. It was incomprehensible to him. In fact, he was tempted to take his blade and pry the blasted thing open right now, payment for services be damned.

But he wasn't a connoisseur like the sheik, who had been pacing around the pedestal the urn now occupied for the past five minutes, saying nothing.

"So, you're not going to open it?"

Khalid stopped in mid-step and stared at him, aghast. "Are you insane? This will never be opened. Why would I spoil the surprise? The wonder? The excitement of possessing it is theorizing over the endless possibilities of what it contains. Not knowing is more exciting than knowing."

"And you aren't dying to find out what's inside?"

"Of course I am. That's the fun of it."

"And when you tire of the fun?"

"Then I'll sell it to someone else."

"Without opening it first?"

Khalid shrugged. "Who knows? Perhaps I'll open it to satisfy my curiosity, then reseal it so that the next owner can have the same enjoyment I have had."

"But he'd know you knew."

"Oh, I'd never tell him. Why deprive him of the satisfaction? After all, he could be a friend of mine."

Tankov shook his head. "I think you're all a little insane."

Khalid glared at him. "Don't let your ignorance interfere with your good judgment. Insulting me can be dangerous for your health."

Tankov regarded him for a moment. "I've insulted far more powerful men than you, and I'm still here to do the same to you."

Khalid seethed, his face red and his fists clenched. It was clear the man wasn't over having been betrayed by the Suqut Brigade, something Tankov hadn't bothered to set him straight on, and was still pissed about having had to call in his team, despite having told him they were finished doing business together less than a week ago.

And Tankov didn't care. He was tired of the sheik, and he had proven he was now a dangerous man by his dealings with the Suqut Brigade. Perhaps it was time to end things.

"You dare insult me in my own home? Do you have any idea who I am?"

Tankov smiled. "I think all the inbreeding in your royal line has caught up to your branch of the House of Saud."

Khalid roared in anger then pointed at the door. "Get out! I never want to see you again! And be thankful that I don't kill you where you stand!"

Tankov bowed his head slightly. "As you wish." He headed for the door then paused, thinking of Professor Acton, who had undoubtedly deciphered his hint when handing over the phone. He took in the Amber Room one last time, then decided to give Acton one last bit of help. "I'm going to give you a friendly warning, for old time's sake."

Khalid glared at him, saying nothing.

"In all the confusion, I lost my cellphone that I had here last time."

Khalid's eyes narrowed. "So?"

"So, if it fell into the wrong hands, they might find out about this place." He smiled slightly. "Something to think about."

Tankov left the room, closing the doors after him as a roar of rage erupted.

Now let's see if the professor's contacts are watching.

Operations Center 2, CIA Headquarters
Langley, Virginia

Sonya Tong expertly manipulated the cameras on the drone deployed over Sheik Khalid's compound outside of Riyadh. "Well, whatever happened in that meeting sure rattled him."

Randy Child, the whiz-kid on Leroux's team, spun in his chair, staring at the ceiling of the Operations Center. "Or he's just moving to a bigger palace."

Leroux stared at the screen, scratching his chin. After receiving Acton's call, he had tasked his team to gather intel on the location, and begin monitoring it, while he put together a briefing for his boss. They had been given approval for a surveillance operation, and were quickly rewarded with a visit just hours ago by a lone man carrying a package that could be large enough to contain the urn Acton had described to him in a follow-up conversation. That visitor had left minutes later, without the package, then a flurry of phone calls were made from the estate. Soon, large transport trucks arrived with packing materials and crews that had been working for hours, each truck leaving after it was loaded.

"I wish there was some way we could know if it was the Amber Room," muttered Kane, standing beside him. "Like Randy said, he could just be moving."

Leroux pursed his lips. "The crates being used match the type and size that the Nazis used. I wouldn't be surprised if they're the same ones." He snapped his fingers. "Zoom in as close as you can on one of those rectangular crates.

Sonya complied and brought up a freezeframe of one of the crates.

With a Nazi swastika on full display.

Leroux grinned at Kane. "I guess that settles that."

Kane shook his head. "The professor is going to love this. Do we know where those trucks are headed?"

Sonya brought up the feed from another drone, an airfield displayed with a large transport aircraft sitting on the tarmac, crews loading it with the contents of one of the trucks.

"Okay, he's not moving to a new palace. At least not in Saudi." Kane scratched his chin. "Any flight plan filed for that thing?"

Child shook his head. "Not that I've been able to find, but there will be if he's leaving their airspace." He pointed at a large crate being loaded. "You know, some of this stuff doesn't match the Amber Room crates. I'm thinking he's moving his entire collection, not just the room."

Leroux nodded in agreement. "It makes sense. He'd be concerned about the Amber Room, as I'm sure it's his prize possession, but he'd likely take the opportunity to save everything. Perhaps even Cylon's urn."

Randy spun again. "Cylon. Sooo cool!"

Leroux turned to him. "Keep monitoring that plane. I want to know the moment it takes off, and where it's headed. Since the Polish government asked for our assistance a few months ago in recovering it, and we failed, according to the director, it's still an open op. Delta already has Bravo Team on standby, in theater, and depending on where that plane lands, we might be able to take it."

Kane pursed his lips, staring at the display. "Let's hope it's someplace we don't care about offending the locals."

Aviano Air Base, Italy

Command Sergeant Major Burt "Big Dog" Dawson entered the room, his team of special operators, all members of 1st Special Forces Operational Detachment-Delta, or Delta Force to the common folk, spread about on various chairs and couches, a few playing a game of pool. Everyone turned expectantly.

"What's up, dog?" asked Sergeant Carl "Niner" Sung. "Are we on?"

Dawson nodded. "It looks like we're getting a second shot at that Amber Room."

Sergeant Leon "Atlas" James' impossibly deep voice boomed from the pool table. "You mean that big ass gold room that the Doc and his lady found?"

Niner stared at him. "Hey, she has a name." He grinned. "That will eventually be Mrs. Sung once the Doc's out of the picture."

"Keep dreaming shit ball."

"With the way you treat me, sometimes all I have are my dreams."

Atlas stared at him. "As long as I don't feature in them, then we're okay."

"Well, there was this one where you were naked except for a flak jacket and a pair of panties—"

"You're dreaming about me, yet you want to marry the Doc's wife. You're confused, little man." Atlas jabbed a meaty finger at Niner. "And don't let the Doc hear you talk like that. It could get your ass capped."

Niner nodded. "He does scare me. He can shoot, oozes sex appeal—"

"I'll bow to your expertise in that area."

"Hey, don't misinterpret the message. All I'm saying is he has to be sexy to women to get the one he's got. She's a stunner, funny—"

"And can kick your ass."

Niner swooned, with a mock dreamy expression. "I know, that's her most attractive quality. A woman that can deliver an ass-whooping. What a way to go!"

Atlas' eyes narrowed. "When was the last time you were laid? And not by the hand twins."

Niner stared at him for a moment, stammering to find a response.

Atlas and the others laughed. "Uh huh. I thought it was that long. You really need to get out and work off some of that built up energy. Your brain is getting stupider by the day."

Niner dove across the pool table and leaped into Atlas' arms like a bride being carried over the threshold. "Are you offering?"

Atlas dumped him unceremoniously on the floor. "You're not my type."

Dawson shook his head then turned as the door opened, a corporal entering with a message. He handed it to Dawson then left. Dawson read it, a smile spreading. "Well, if you ladies are done, we have a destination."

Atlas stepped over Niner, placing a boot on his chest in the process. "A fun one?"

Dawson grinned. "Oh yeah."

Ghardabiya Airbase, Libya

"Zero-One in position."

Dawson stared through his night vision goggles at the Libyan airbase in front of him as Atlas cut the wires of the fence. The team had just HALO jumped from thirty thousand feet, and were now deployed in three teams with Niner and his spotter Sergeant Gerry "Jimmy Olsen" Hudson, as a sniper team providing them with cover from a nearby hilltop.

The sheik's plane was a couple of hundred yards away, its engines winding down, as crews rushed from a nearby hangar, crews that, judging by their equipment, intended to offload the cargo.

"Why would he leave it here?" asked Atlas as they pushed through the new opening in the fence.

Dawson shook his head. "I'm guessing he thinks this is the last place we'd look."

Atlas grunted. "He's right. A failed state is hardly where I'd expect to find a priceless art collection."

Dawson activated his comm. "Okay, gentlemen, that's our ride, and we want the cargo, so let's hit them before they get a chance to unload. Everyone in position?"

"Team Two in position," replied Master Sergeant Mike "Red" Belme, from the north end of the field.

"Team Three in position," echoed Sergeant Will "Spock" Lightman from the southern end.

Dawson surveyed the area once again for any surprises, then signaled the attack. "Execute-Execute-Execute!" He jumped to his feet, surging forward, hunched over, his team on his heels as they advanced as silently as they could, suppressed MP5s at the ready. Dawson glanced to his left then right, spotting both teams, when his eyes narrowed. "What the hell is that?"

Atlas caught up. "What?"

"Check north."

Atlas looked and cursed. "I think it's the hand of God."

Dawson activated his comm, not breaking stride. "Control, Zero-One. Care to let us in on what's coming in from the north, over?"

"Zero-One, Control. You've got a sandstorm coming in."

Dawson cursed. "ETA?"

"Less than ten minutes."

Dawson shook his head, glancing at Atlas. "Might have been nice to know."

Atlas grinned. "I'm sure they just didn't want us worrying."

Dawson raised his weapon, taking aim at the cluster of hostiles when one of them shouted. "We've been made." He squeezed the trigger, his weapon set to single shot, and made quick work of those in his arc as the rest of his team did the same. Red's team to the north was taking heavier fire, but Dawson let his best friend and second-in-command deal with it rather than interrupt him with a status update request. Gunfire from the south had him more concerned, the distinct sound of a .50 caliber opening up on Spock's team, now dominating the field.

He pointed toward Team Three's position. "Jagger, Mickey, give them a hand."

Jagger and Mickey split off, rushing the defenders' position from behind, as Dawson, Atlas, and their pilot extraordinaire, Sergeant Zack "Wings" Hauser, continued toward the massive transport aircraft.

An aircraft whose engines were now powering up once again.

"He's going to try and make a break for it." Wings poured on the speed as Dawson opened fire on a new set of guards emerging from the hangar. The aircraft's lowered ramp slowly rose, and once closed, there'd be no Tom Cruise style entrance through the side door, because Scotty wasn't on the next ridge miraculously hacking into the plane's automated systems to open it.

It would be another failed mission to recover the half-billion dollar historical treasure.

"Bullshit."

Dawson sprinted as hard as he could, switching over to fully automatic, spraying the area with lead as Atlas and Wings did the same. It kept their enemies' heads down, and their returned fire unaimed.

Dawson leaped, grabbing the lip of the cargo ramp, then flipped over the edge, rolling hard to the deck. Somebody yelled as they charged at him, always a stupid thing to do, giving him enough warning to unload two rounds into the man's stomach, then advance, using him as a meat shield as he advanced through the hold, eliminating the three men still inside.

He tossed the bullet-ridden corpse to the side and checked behind him to see he was alone, the others too slow. He smacked the button to lower the ramp, then made for the cockpit. It was locked, and the plane was still picking up speed despite the ramp lowering.

He placed a small charge on the lock and blew it as Atlas and Wings reached him. Atlas hauled the door off its hinges then Dawson and Wings stepped into the cockpit, both with weapons aimed at the crews' heads.

"How about we stop this thing?"

The pilot powered down and they unbuckled themselves. Dawson and Atlas hauled them out of the cockpit and toward the rear ramp, Wings once again lowering it, the crew having overridden it from their position.

Dawson tossed the pilot down the ramp as the rest of his team sprinted inside. "Everybody good?"

Red nodded. "All present and accounted for, but I spotted three technicals on their way. We better book."

Dawson did a headcount as the rest got on board, then activated his comm. "Overseer, time to fly."

Niner responded. "Way ahead of you, Zero-One."

Dawson turned back toward the cockpit. "Let's pick up Niner and get the hell out of here!"

The wind was beginning to howl, sand whipping past them as Dawson raised the ramp. He pointed toward the side door. "Open that." Spock and Jagger immediately opened it, taking up position on either side to retrieve Niner and Jimmy, as Dawson headed for the cockpit, taking the copilot's position. He took a look through the window and his eyes bulged. "Holy shit!"

Wings grunted. "No shit holy shit! We've got maybe two minutes."

Dawson scanned the end of the runway, visibility already poor, then pointed. "That's them."

Wings nodded, guiding the plane toward their remaining two team members, Niner waving with a shit eating grin, shouting something at them that he thought was funny.

Wings shook his head. "That guy really does need to get laid."

His two team members disappeared and Dawson turned to watch the retrieval through the cockpit door. A sniper rifle appeared, tossed through the side door, then Jimmy stumbled inside, and finally Niner, rolling onto his back, still laughing. The side door closed, and Wings turned the plane hard, aligning them for takeoff.

"Everybody hang on, this ain't gonna be pretty!"

Dawson strapped in as the others in the rear searched for something to hold on to, the stolen art collection taking up most of the hold.

Wings shoved the throttle forward and the plane surged as the wind and sand whipped around them. The runway ahead was shrouded in a writhing cloud of unforgiving sand, and Dawson found himself checking over his shoulder to make sure the engines were okay.

"Hang on!"

Wings pulled back on the stick and the nose lifted, then the rear wheels, cheers erupting from the back of the plane. Dawson breathed a sigh of relief as Wings continued to focus, struggling with the controls.

Suddenly the storm cleared and there was nothing but pristine night sky ahead of them, Wings visibly relaxing, banking them to port.

Jimmy appeared in the hatch. "Everything good?"

Wings nodded. "Yup."

Dawson looked back at the others. "What was Niner laughing about?"

Jimmy shook his head. "Oh, something about how this is what happens when Atlas farts in the desert. You know how he gets with fart jokes."

Dawson chuckled. "He really does need to get laid." He slapped Wings on the shoulder. "Good flying. Next stop, Poland."

Wings tapped the fuel gauge. "Umm, we might want to hit a Texaco. We're kind of low on gas."

Lask Air Base

Lask, Poland

Acton gave Laura an excited shake as the large transport aircraft came to a stop and the engines began to power down. He was pretty confident about what was on board, but nothing had been confirmed yet. All he knew was that he had received a message from Kane to be here, at this time.

"Do you think they have it?"

Acton grinned at Laura. "They have to! Look at the size of that thing."

The ramp lowered and a group of familiar faces were soon descending, broad smiles all around.

"BD!" Acton extended his hand when Niner blasted past him, shoving him out of the way, and giving Laura a bearhug.

"Hiya, darlin'!"

Laura returned the hug, laughing. "Niner, not in front of James. He'll get jealous!"

Niner grinned. "Let him!"

Acton shook Dawson's hand, then they both headed for the ramp. "Well? I'm dying to know."

Dawson smiled. "We did some poking around while we were in transit, and according to Professor Google, there are a lot of things in here that you won't be expecting."

"The Amber Room. Is it there?"

Dawson paused dramatically, then nodded. "Yes, it is."

Acton turned back toward Laura, his fists pumping the air as she leaped into his arms, hugging him hard. He turned to Professor Aleksandra Lisowski, who had nearly died when the precious artifact had first been discovered only a few months ago. "Aleksandra, it's here!"

She was bouncing with joy too, already on her phone, probably letting the Polish authorities know the good news.

Dawson stepped into the hold of the aircraft and pointed at a crate. "There's something else here you might be interested in." He popped the already loosened top off then stepped back. Acton looked inside, then carefully unwrapped the bundle, his heart hammering harder and harder as he anticipated what it might be.

The blanket fell away and he gasped. "Cylon's urn!"

Dawson seemed pleased with his excitement. "It's the only thing that we found that matched the description you gave us. So, what's so special about it?"

Acton gave them the executive summary of what was known, and what had happened in Athens, leaving the Bravo Team members shaking their heads once more at the incidents they constantly managed to get themselves into.

Niner warily looked inside. "And you say this thing has a curse written on it?"

"Yup." Acton frowned. "You know, pretty much everyone who's come into contact with this thing has been killed, kidnapped, or arrested." He stepped back. "Maybe it's better to be safe than sorry."

Niner shook his head. "I wouldn't worry about it, Doc. There's no way your luck could possibly get any worse."

Acton laughed. "I agree." He stared at the crate, becoming somber. "I do wonder, though, how it all happened. What made Cylon write what he did, and was it him that died in the necropolis all those years ago?"

Laura came up beside him, wrapping an arm around him. "I guess we'll never know."

He squeezed her. "But it is fun to speculate."

Outside the Necropolis

632 BC

Cylon stepped from the shadows of the final resting place of so many that had meant so much to him, and sprinted across the open field toward the cover of the nearby buildings. He reached an alleyway and came to a halt, steadying his heavy breathing and listening for any signs of pursuit.

None.

He glanced over his shoulder at the sliver of light on the horizon. It would soon be daylight, and life would return to these now empty streets, a few carts already underway as shopkeepers prepared for their early morning customers.

Covered in blood, he would make quite the spectacle.

He only had minutes to escape to the countryside and find shelter from the sun while he plotted the death of the man responsible for the horrors that had befallen his comrades.

Megacles.

The archon had to know he would be coming for him, so he would likely have increased the number of guards surrounding him. It might take some doing to get close, but Cylon did have an advantage over most would-be assassins.

He was willing to die to accomplish his goal.

He winced at the forgotten amulet cutting into his palm, his grip so tight it was close to drawing blood. He opened his fingers and stared at the gift that had given him so much hope. Yet he had conveniently ignored the full breadth of what Pythia had said.

"Wear this to give you the strength of Apollo. Should you succeed, blessed will be all who wear it. But should you fail, all who possess it shall know nothing but misery."

He had failed, spectacularly, and he now knew nothing but misery, and Basileios, who had also possessed it, was now dead, suffering a horrible, painful, prolonged death.

Pythia had been right.

And so wrong.

No, that was you.

He had chosen poorly.

If only you had listened to Basileios. He was right, it wasn't the Olympics.

He growled, hurling the amulet into the middle of the street, then set a brisk pace for the outskirts before the light of day revealed his presence.

Somebody shouted behind him, a warning, and he spun to see a young boy rush out into the road and bend over to pick something up, oblivious to the cart barreling toward him. Cylon reached out a hand, futilely, his jaw dropping in horror as the horse and carriage rolled over the young boy, his screams of agony tearing at Cylon's heart as he sprinted toward the carnage, the rear wheel coming to rest on the boy's chest.

And as the first rays of sunlight dawned, Cylon cried out with an anguish he had never before experienced as he recognized the mangled form of his own son, lying under the wheel of that which had crushed him.

With a surge of strength surely provided by Apollo himself, Cylon lifted the fully laden cart off his son's chest, and shoved it on its side. He dropped to his knees, lifting his son, still alive, though fading fast, each gasped breath a little quicker, a little shorter.

"What are you doing here?"

His son's eyes fluttered open. "I-I followed Mother, then you. I-I wanted to see you."

Cylon stared at him, tears streaking his cheeks, as he finally realized the sounds he had been hearing all evening were that of his son's slight frame following him in the shadows.

"If only you had revealed yourself."

His son reached up and grabbed at his beard. "I-I'm sorry I disobeyed you, Father. Don't cry."

Cylon ran his fingers through his son's hair, straightening the messed tresses, forcing a smile when everything told him not to. "It's okay, my son. I forgive you."

"Tell-tell Mother that I…"

His voice faded, replaced with nothing more than a long, shallow sigh, the spark of life that once dominated his deep blue eyes gone.

Cylon roared at the heavens above, damning the gods who would let this happen, damning Apollo, damning Athena, and damning the Oracle herself, as he clasped his son's tiny lifeless body against his own.

A crowd had gathered to watch the misery unfolding, the light of day now filling the streets with long shadows, his name whispered as he was recognized.

There would be no hiding now.

There would be no revenge on Megacles.

There would be no more nights with his wife.

He was already dead inside, cursed by the gods who had lead him down this path of tragedy.

He rose, bending over to pick up his son, when he noticed his tiny hand was tightly clasped, as if gripping something. He opened his son's hand, his heart hammering with the memory of doing the same to his friend's only minutes ago.

And screamed in rage and horror at the sight of the amulet he had tossed into the street.

He was the architect of his own son's demise, the poor foolish boy rushing into the street to grab that which his father had discarded, probably in the hopes of returning it to him one day, the proud son saving his father from a perhaps foolhardy emotional decision.

"Oh, you beautiful, brave child." His shoulders shook with the knowledge that his failure had taken yet another life. He stared at the amulet, truly a curse on the Cylon family, and rose, lifting his son in his arms, his vision blurred with burning tears.

"I'm so sorry, sir, I didn't see him."

Cylon ignored the man who had driven the cart, instead beginning to walk toward the necropolis where his friends lay interred. "Tell Megacles that I, Cylon, await him." He paused, spotting a large jar lying on the ground beside the overturned cart. "Give me that."

The man nodded, grabbing it, and placing it on the chest of Cylon's only child. Nothing was said. There was nothing to say. It had been an accident, arranged by the gods. No one was to blame except Cylon himself, for he had failed, and cursed his family and anyone associated with him, forever.

He entered the necropolis and placed his son's body at the front of the line of his fallen friends along with the jar. He stared at the body of his friend, Basileios, at the far end, then made a decision. With his sword, he broke the chain binding his friend to the others, then carried his lifeless corpse to the front of the line, placing him beside his son. He arranged them both in as peaceful a pose as he could, then removed the lid from the large jar, dropping the amulet inside, then pressing the cover back in place. He retrieved a wax candle from the wall, lighting it with the torch he had left behind earlier, then used the wax to seal the lid in place, as he heard a growing crowd gather outside.

They'll be here soon.

He sat between his son and best friend with the vase, or what he now was certain was an urn, nestled in his lap. He picked up a small stone and began to write on the outside of the jar, a warning to all who might be tempted to retrieve that which it contained.

Cursed be all who possess that which this contains, so sayeth Pythia, Oracle of Apollo.

He stared at what he had written, then decided additional gravitas was required, etching one last word below his warning.

Cylon.

He placed the urn between two of the three most important people in his life, then rose, drawing his sword as the first of his challengers arrived, praying one of them would be Megacles.

He took one last look at his friend, then his son, and smiled.

"I'll be with you soon."

THE END

ACKNOWLEDGMENTS

This book is dedicated to Malcolm Stone. Malcolm was a fan for some time, and reached out to me December 24th, 2014, in response to my annual Christmas email. Over the years, he responded to most of my newsletter emails, and quite quickly we began exchanging emails about many things beyond just the books. I've received emails from his family, and have found them all to have terrific senses of humor, and all to have been devoted to Malcolm.

While writing my last book, I sent an email to a small group of proofreaders, one of whom was Malcolm. He never opened it. I knew he had been ill for some time, and grew concerned. I woke up on the morning of May 20, 2018, and checked once again, deciding that I'd send him an email just to make sure he was okay.

This led to the discovery of a new email that had arrived from his family, telling me of his death the night before.

I found this quite devastating, but was also honored that his family had thought to contact me individually, within hours of his death, to let me know what had happened. I considered Malcolm a friend, though we had never met or even spoken, and I will miss him very much.

I hope he would have loved what you just read, and still thought I "ruled the genre."

I often get asked where I get my ideas from, and this one might be less obvious than you think. I've always been a huge Battlestar Galactica fan. As a kid, when we were stationed in Europe, my grandparents would tape it on VHS (remember that?) and send me episodes. I was immediately hooked. When the reboot came out, I was hooked all over again. I loved the re-imagining, and have watched it countless times.

Those who watched the original series would remember the heavy Ancient Greek influence. Apollo, Athena, the Viper pilot helmets that looked like they were straight out of Ancient Greece. Clearly, the creator Glen A. Larson had been influenced by this, and the concept suggested a relationship between Ancient Earth and the colonies.

I understood all of this, and enjoyed that concept, but never realized that one of the most important aspects of the show came from history as well.

A few months ago, I was in my car, listening to the radio, and they were talking about an archaeological find in Athens—an ancient necropolis. I had heard of this a couple of years ago, but this time they were talking about 80 skeletons they had discovered, many shackled, yet still buried with some semblance of honor.

It intrigued me.

But what really caught my attention was the theory as to who these people could be.

The followers of Cylon.

My jaw dropped, I stared at the radio, and I think I said something like, "Are you f'n kidding me?" Needless to say, I was shocked at this revelation. I had always assumed the term Cylon was something made up by Larson for the TV series. I had figured it was short for Cybernetic "something," but to discover that Cylon was actually a figure from history had me racing home and reading everything I could find.

And a book idea was born.

As usual, there are people to thank. My dad for all the research, Brent Richards for some weapons info, and, as usual, my wife, daughter, and mother, as well as the proofing and launch teams.

As well, I'd like to thank the winners of some contests on my Facebook page, Carolanne Burnett who supplied the name of Leather's new love interest, and Angela Lee who chose the pub Reading and his son were enjoying beers at. To participate in these contests, please follow me on Facebook at:

https://www.facebook.com/jrobertkennedy.

To those who have not already done so, please visit my website at www.jrobertkennedy.com then sign up for the Insider's Club to be notified of new book releases. Your email address will never be shared or sold, and you'll only receive the occasional email from me, as I don't have time to spam you!

Thank you once again for reading.

Made in the USA
Las Vegas, NV
05 September 2021